THE LAST LEAP

When respected businessman Alvin Day fell to his death from San Francisco's Golden Gate Bridge, his widow refused to accept the suicide verdict. Suspecting murder, she called in Dale Shand. It turned out to be murder all right — but with a macabre difference. Four people were to die violently before Dale cracked this most bizarre case wide open, in a climactic showdown on the spot where it all began — the bridge.

Books by Douglas Enefer
in the Linford Mystery Library:

THE DEADLY STREAK

DOUGLAS ENEFER

THE
LAST LEAP

Complete and Unabridged

LINFORD
Leicester

First published in Great Britain in 1983 by
Robert Hale Limited
London

First Linford Edition
published January 1995
by arrangement with
Robert Hale Limited
London

British Library CIP Data

Enefer, Douglas
The last leap.—Large print ed.—
Linford mystery library
I. Title II. Series
823.914 [F]

ISBN 0-7089-7644-1

Published by
F. A. Thorpe (Publishing) Ltd.
Anstey, Leicestershire

Set by Words & Graphics Ltd.
Anstey, Leicestershire
Printed and bound in Great Britain by
T. J. Press (Padstow) Ltd., Padstow, Cornwall

This book is printed on acid-free paper

1,

THE house stood on a gentle knoll over in Pasadena. A two-storey brownstone house you'd be more likely to encounter in the East Seventies of New York City. Maybe it had been dug up by the roots and transported bodily across the continent? Madder things happened in Southern California.

I put my rented Dodge compact on the rolled gravel drive, got out and thumbed the doorbell. The door opened and I was looking at a small Mexican girl in a maid's uniform.

"Mr Dale Shand?" Her soft voice complemented her deep brown eyes.

I nodded. She held the door wide open. "You are expected, *señor* — please come in."

I followed her across a tiled hallway into a wide, comfortably furnished room. The woman who came forward to meet me was in her mid-thirties, tall and elegantly slim with burnished coppery hair worn long to her shoulders.

"I'm so glad you were able to come, Mr Shand." She held out a smooth hand. "Would you like coffee — or perhaps you would prefer something stronger?"

"Coffee will be fine."

"Anita will bring some. Won't you sit down?"

I lowered myself into a chintz-covered armchair and said: "I'm in California on a three-week vacation and looked up Charles Forbes whom I used to know when he was practising law in New York. That was years ago. Since then I've made my home in London."

"So I understand. Charles is my attorney. He tells me that you have been very successful in England." Larraine Day promoted a brief smile on her oval face. I had a momentary impression that she hadn't smiled much lately.

2

She went on: "You apparently impressed him — which is not the easiest thing to do. Actually, Charles was not wildly in favour of me engaging a private investigator, but he said that if I insisted you were the best. He also mentioned that you were likely to be the most expensive."

The maid wheeled in the coffee. I stirred mine and said levelly: "Forbes didn't go into details — he preferred that I get them directly from you — but I gather that you want me to investigate the circumstances of your husband's death."

For a long moment she sat in silence with her hands folded in her lap. Finally, she said: "I want you to find out who killed my husband."

I put my cup and saucer down on a beaten copper side table. "Are you telling me that you think he was murdered?"

"Yes . . ."

"Homicide is police business, Mrs Day."

3

"Yes, I know. Charles was at pains to point that out to me."

"A private investigator who tangles with homicide is likely to find himself in trouble with the law. You must know that, Mrs Day."

"The circumstances are exceptional, Mr Shand. The police are satisfied that my husband committed suicide — I am not."

It was my turn to fall silent. Thoughts moved in my mind: a man gets dead, the cops say he took his own life, his widow has the crazy notion that somebody killed him — only Larraine Day doesn't look even halfway to being crazy. I could sense my interest kindling.

"I guess you'd better tell the story without interruption from me," I said.

"You mean you'll take the case?"

"You're moving a little fast, Mrs Day. "Right now I'm willing to listen. I'll decide about handling it or not later. I think that's fair."

"Yes," she said. "Yes, it is.

Incidentally, I appreciate your giving me your time while on holiday."

She paused, as if assembling facts in her mind. Then she resumed: "I married Alvin ten years ago. I was then twenty-five. He was twelve years older than me and at that time was the junior partner in a realty business. When the senior partner passed on Alvin moved up and acquired full control of the business. So there was no reason for him to contemplate taking his own life."

"It doesn't necessarily follow."

"If you mean money troubles you can dismiss that thought, Mr Shand. The company's affairs were in perfect order. I have already had three excellent offers for the business — and, in addition, I inherit a hundred thousand dollars in cash, plus investments."

"There could be other reasons for suicide, reasons apart from financial ones."

"You mean trouble involving a woman, I take it?"

"I don't want to seem brutal — but it's a possibility, isn't it?"

"No!" The word came out flatly.

"You sound very positive."

"I'd have known. A woman always knows."

"Not always. Some men can be very adept at concealing a fact like that."

"I'd have known," she repeated.

I didn't say anything.

"I thought you were going to listen without interruption," she stormed.

"I apologize — please tell it in your own words."

"Thank you." Her contralto voice mellowed. "We had a very agreeable marriage. Perhaps even placid. Alvin was at the office all day and at home every night. We had shared interests — music, reading, tennis, watching television and periodically entertaining friends. Alvin rarely made out-of-town business trips, he preferred to be at home. He quite literally gave himself no opportunities to form a clandestine attachment. On the rare occasions when he had to spend a night or two away from home he called me regularly on the telephone — twice in a single night."

I finished my coffee, still not saying anything.

Larraine Day said: "In the last seven months Alvin was never away from our home until three weeks ago when he had to see a client in San Francisco. He never came back . . . "

"Are you saying he died there at that time?"

A small shiver possessed her. "Yes, that's where it happened."

"What exactly happened, Mrs Day?"

"Alvin arranged to spend two nights in San Francisco. On the second night he didn't call me. I waited until ten o'clock, then I telephoned his hotel. He wasn't there and nobody knew where he was likely to be. I was frantic. I had a sort of premonition that something had happened to him . . . "

She took a king-size cigarette from a cedarwood box. I flared my lighter for her while she took a long inhalation. Then she said: "In desperation I called the police, the San Francisco police. But I had nothing to go on and they didn't seem very interested. They said husbands frequently disappeared, but that if he didn't turn up I could contact the Missing Persons Bureau.

"The next day I flew to San Francisco after finding out that he hadn't been back to his hotel — the Ocean Point Inn it was. I stayed there two nights. I was half out of my mind with anxiety. I went to the Missing Persons Bureau. They were very polite and took all the details, but they didn't seem optimistic.

"I went back home, called all Alvin's business associates and our personal friends. Nobody could tell me anything. A week passed, the most dreadful week I can ever remember . . ."

She mashed her unfinished cigarette out in a crystal ash tray and said: "The week went by. Then I got a telephone call from the San Francisco police. They said Alvin's body had been taken from the sea, that he had committed suicide by jumping from the Golden Gate Bridge."

"I'm sorry." The words sounded trite in my own ears. "What did they base the suicide theory on?"

"After the body was found someone came forward and said something about seeing my husband on the bridge, acting as if he was about to jump off it."

"Someone who recognized him?"

Larraine Day shook her head. "It wasn't as specific as that — at least not at first. A man told the police about seeing this man on the bridge looking as if he was going to jump. Then sea mist blotted out the view and when it cleared the man was no longer on the bridge. When the police recovered my husband's body the other man recognized him by his clothes . . . I'm telling this in a muddled kind of way, aren't I?"

"It's clear enough, Mrs Day. A man sees another man on the bridge acting like he's about to leap from it. He

9

doesn't actually see him do it on account of the mist, but when the body is found he claims he could identify the clothing. Question — was your husband wearing distinctive clothing?"

"I don't know that you could call it distinctive. Alvin was wearing a navy blue mohair blazer and light grey slacks, a white shirt with a button-down collar — oh, and a dark blue tie with slim white stripes."

"The colours of Eton College, England."

"Are they? I didn't know that. But there's no connection. I mean Alvin didn't go to Eton."

"I imagine not, but the point is that your husband owned clothes like that?"

"Yes, he bought them only recently in Los Angeles at a small shop off Wilshire Boulevard."

"And the onlooker recognized the clothes when the body was found? I'm taking it that he didn't actually see your husband's face?"

"No, he said Alvin's back was turned. Then the sea mist came down and when it cleared there was no sign of him."

"Did you identify the body, Mrs Day?"

She shook her head. "No, the police said it was showing signs of decomposition . . . I couldn't bear to see it, so the identification was done by George Lane, my husband's office manager."

"I don't want to distress you, Mrs Day — but why should anyone want to kill your husband?"

"I can't answer that, I simply don't know. That's why I want you to act for me. *Please*."

"Are you saying that under cover of sudden mist someone deliberately pushed him off the bridge?"

"I've no proof, but there can't be any other explanation. I just *know* that Alvin didn't throw himself off."

"He would have to be in a position from which he could be pushed over," I said.

"I've thought of that. He could have been looking over the rails."

"It's possible — but why should he be on the bridge at all?"

"He could have been taking an evening stroll — people do walk on to the bridge."

"And a total stranger pushes him off it — or maybe not a stranger."

She looked startled. "I hadn't thought of that . . . "

"Somebody who knew him, somebody who wished him ill. Or somebody with a deranged mind. A stranger, a homicidal maniac — a psycho."

She made another small shiver. "I don't know, but Alvin was murdered — I'm sure of it."

"Did you say that to the police?"

"Yes, to a detective lieutenant from the San Francisco police named Bakso."

"What did *he* say?"

"He was quite courteous but he insisted that there was no evidence of murder and that they were satisfied that Alvin committed suicide." Her mouth twitched faintly. "I got the impression that he thought I was imagining things. Is that what *you* think, Mr Shand?"

I looked at her directly.

"No," I said.

"You believe me, you believe that Alvin was murdered?"

"I can't go that far, not yet — but I believe that *you* believe it."

"What does that mean?"

"Just that I'll take the case."

"Thank you," she said in a small voice.

"You can thank me on completion — or not."

"You mean . . . " She left the rest of the sentence unfinished.

"The investigation may confirm the police view — you have to face that possibility."

For a long moment she didn't answer. Then she said composedly: "I'll take that risk, but I don't believe it will be like that. It's something I *feel* inside me."

She rose, crossed the room and came

back with a framed photograph, head and shoulders. It showed a dark-haired man in early middle age, a man with a strong composed face.

Larraine Day said: "My husband — is that the picture of a man who would take his own life?"

I took the picture from her, studying it. "No," I said, "but a man can act out of character under strain."

"I'm certain it wasn't like that." She hesitated. "What will you do?"

"See your husband's business associates and friends. I'll need a list, but first I'll need to make an on-the-spot assessment. I want to visit the scene — see where it actually happened. It may or may not yield something. But that's where I start."

"You'll go to San Francisco?"

"Today," I said.

★ ★ ★

I drove back to L.A. and went straight to Forbes's office. He rose from behind

14

an unlittered executive desk, a tall amiable man with a thick cluster of iron grey hair, and said: "Well?"

"I've agreed to handle the inquiry. I'm not saying I go along with her theory, or not yet, but I'm willing to look into it."

"It's enough that you're taking the case, Dale — and it's appreciated. What did you make of Larraine?"

"A woman of looks and charm who clearly believes that her husband didn't take his life. Her sincerity impressed me — but it could still turn out to be no more than an erroneous belief."

"Did you say that to her?"

"I told her she had to face that possibility. She was willing to take the risk."

"I'm assuming that you'll want to go to San Francisco right away."

"On the earliest possible flight."

"No problem." He slid open a desk drawer and took out a manila envelope.

I grinned. "So you've already got the tickets?"

"In anticipation of your taking the case."

"What if I hadn't?"

"There'd have been time to cancel the booking and get a refund. But I was pretty damn sure you'd take the case."

"There's one difficulty — I don't have a licence to work over here as a private eye."

"No problem again. I've got you temporary cover both in Los Angeles and San Francisco. I have a friendly relationship with the D.A. in both cities. I've written down names to contact should that become necessary."

"Thanks — I don't want to run foul of the law on this visit to my native land."

Forbes pushed back an impeccable shirt cuff to look at his gold wrist watch and said: "You're booked on the fourteen hundred hours flight. That gives us time for lunch at a very good steak house I know near the airport. Let's go."

We were at the coffee stage when he said: "About your fee — did you discuss it with Larraine?"

"No, but she said she understood I was expensive."

"I told her that. She will pay your daily rate, however high it is — plus a substantial completion bonus."

"Meaning if the investigation confirms her theory?"

"Either way," Forbes said.

2

THE plane came in on time at San Francisco and I took a taxi to the police precinct station which had handled the case.

A clerk in civilian clothes looked up inquiringly and said: "Yeah?"

"Dale Shand calling on Detective Lieutenant Bakso, if he's in."

"He expecting you, Mr Shand?"

"No, but he'll probably want to see me if you tell him I'm representing Mrs Larraine Day, the widow of the man who fell off the Golden Gate bridge recently."

"Oh, that guy." The clerk put a wad of chewing-gum in his mouth and added: "The way I got the picture he jumped off it."

"Jumped or fell — one or the other, or not."

The clerk moved the gum from

one side of his mouth to the other, eyeing me. He seemed about to say something in reply, then changed his mind and reached for the internal telephone. "The lieutenant's in — I'll tell him you're here, Mr Shand."

He dialled a number. "A Mr Dale Shand wants to see you, Lieutenant. Says he's representing the widow of the fellow who jumped off the Golden Gate Bridge. The fellow named Day."

There was a short pause. Then he cradled the receiver and said: "The lieutenant will see you, Mr Shand — first door on the right down the corridor." He nodded in the direction.

"Thanks." I went down the corridor and into a small cluttered office. A man stood up behind a desk. A scrawny man with stiff brownish hair and hard blue eyes. He was wearing an oatmeal sport jacket over tan slacks. They looked expensive.

"What can I do for you, Mr Shand?" The gritty voice matched the hardness of the eyes.

"You may be able to save me some trouble, Lieutenant."

"I don't get it," he said.

"I mean our conversation could make any further inquiries by me unnecessary."

"What inquiries?"

I said evenly: "Mrs Larraine Day asked me to look into the circumstances of her husband's death."

"She did? You her attorney?"

"I'm a private investigator."

"Let's see your licence."

"I don't have a licence in the normal sense, but I do have a temporary authorization to operate both in Los Angeles and San Francisco." I showed the documentation Forbes had got for me.

Bakso read it through twice, then poked it back across the desk. "I see your permanent place of residence is London, England, but that you're still a citizen of the United States. How's that?"

"I'm over here on a vacation." I

explained the circumstances briefly, adding: "I called on Charles Forbes whom I used to know when he was a lawyer in New York. He asked me, as a favour, to see Mrs Day."

"And Forbes gets you temporary cover to work here. I don't necessarily have to tell you anything, though."

"That's right, but I'd appreciate it if we could have a friendly chat, Lieutenant."

Bakso flipped a cigarette from a new pack, lit it and waved the match up and down until the small flame died. He seemed to be pondering. Finally, he said: "I suppose she tried to sell you the idea that her old man was murdered?"

"She said he wasn't the kind of man who would take his own life."

"Any kind of man will take his own life in certain circumstances. This one did." Bakso exhaled a long thin smoke stream and went on: "She's got it into her head that he was pushed off the bridge, but the facts don't bear it out. I went to a lot of trouble looking into that angle and came up with nothing. You can take it for sure that Day threw himself off the bridge."

"All the circumstances pointed to suicide?"

"Sure did. Look — there isn't even the shadow of a doubt. I couldn't locate a single witness to anything even slightly pointing to murder."

Bakso paused. "I take it you know about the bridge and all the guys jumping off it?"

"I've heard about it, Lieutenant."

"Forty odd years since the Golden Gate Bridge was opened and the tally of suicides now stands at more than six hundred." Bakso grinned. "Back in 1972 a death-watch began for the five hundredth jump. Sure enough, some young guy walks on to the bridge with the number five hundred clipped to his shirt back, like he was an athlete. He and thirteen others were hauled off at the last moment — but four weeks later somebody else made it."

Bakso mashed his cigarette out in a tin tray piled with stubs and said: "It's a two hundred and sixty-three foot drop and it takes three seconds before they hit the water at eighty mph. At that speed it's like hitting solid concrete from the twenty-third floor of a skyscraper. They die of multiple injuries. You know sump'n — they all choose the east side of the bridge. On the west is the open Pacific — and the sharks. Not that they avoid the sharks. The bodies drift out to sea on the seven mph current where the sharks await them."

"I thought the authorities had TV cameras as spotters."

"Well, yeah, that's right. For each one that jumps off the bridge four are yanked from the rails by guards scanning the closed circuit television. The cameras have cut the number of suicides, but they still try. Like Alvin Day — and he might've been pulled back but for the sudden mist."

"You're confident there wasn't any foul play?"

"Sure. Incidentally, when his body was recovered it had been sliced by the sharks." Bakso set fire to another cigarette. "Wasn't pretty . . . just as well his wife didn't do the identification."

"I guess it was. Does she know about what the sharks did?"

"We kind of spared her the gruesome details. A young fellow named George Lane, Day's office manager, came up and saw the body."

I said meditatively, "It's four to one against any one person pulling off a successful suicide — why choose that way out?"

"There's some powerful attraction about it, I guess. Well, there must be with so many doing it."

"Alvin Day must have had a reason — did you find a motive, Lieutenant?"

Bakso shook his head. "No apparent motive. It certainly wasn't money — I gather he left his widow well provided for, as they say."

"There has to be a reason, though."

"It could be anything."

"Like what?"

"Blackmail, for instance. We've no evidence, but you asked about a possible reason and that could be it."

"Blackmail over what?"

Bakso didn't answer directly. He said: "I guess you know they call this city the gay capital of the United States."

"Are you saying he was a homosexual and was being blackmailed because of it?"

"I'm not saying he *was*. I'm only saying it's a possibility. Seven hundred thousand people live in San Francisco and it's been estimated that about a hundred thousand are queer. Day could of got involved. Not that we've any evidence that he was, and the way things are right now we don't seem likely to. But, for whatever hidden reason, he jumped off the bridge all right. That's for sure — he was seen acting suspiciously before the mist rolled in from the sea."

"So I gather — some man who happened to be on or very near the spot, wasn't it?"

"That's right, a young guy who was out walking. He made a statement."

"Any objection to me seeing him?"

"There could be. This is police business and the department wouldn't give the big hello to a private dick muscling in — more especially if he's trying to make a homicide case out of a straight suicide."

"I wouldn't be doing that if he was merely a witness to a suicide. Besides, I don't necessarily believe that Day was murdered — I'm simply trying to set his wife's mind at rest."

"It *was* suicide — everything points to it." Bakso grinned. "As to the witness, he was a visitor, staying here several weeks. If you want to see him you'll have to go to New York. He stayed on for the coroner's inquiry — we had to insist on that — then he went back east."

"Would asking for his name and address be too much?"

"Strictly speaking, yeah. On the other hand I'm willing to bend the rules just this once. He gave his name as Albert Fisher, c/o the Humbert Arms, Delaney Street, Greenwich Village, NYC."

"Thanks."

"It's a small hotel. He said he had been living there some time before coming out to San Francisco on some business. We didn't check it out on account of all we wanted from him was his eye-witness statement. He said he had been planning to move to Chicago shortly. He may already have gone. He told us he was negotiating for a job there. But even if you saw him he wouldn't be able to add to what he told us."

"I guess not — and I don't particularly want to go to New York."

"You'd be wasting your time and your client's money. We can save you that by letting you see the full statement he made to us. A bit irregular, but it can be done."

He opened a drawer and brought out a foolscap-size buff folder, sliding it across the desk. I read the statement rapidly. It reduced to the simple fact that Albert Fisher claimed to have seen a man, subsequently identified as Alvin Day, climbing the rails on the Golden Gate Bridge at 8 p.m. on the night in question, that a sudden mist blotted him from view and that when it lifted he was no longer there. The statement added that the witness heard the sound of a body hitting the water and that the said Albert Fisher immediately alerted the bridge guards.

Bakso said: "We considered the possibility of murder. We went to a lot of trouble checking it out. All our inquiries substantiate that Day was alone and that he threw himself off the bridge."

I said: "It seems conclusive enough."

"Yeah, a guy doesn't start to climb the bridge parapet unless he's on the brink of suicide. We were satisfied."

The key question was what actually happened during the time mist blotted out the view, but I kept the thought to myself.

Aloud I said: "Well, thanks for talking to me, Lieutenant. I appreciate it as a friendly departure from the normal police attitude towards a private operator — an attitude which I used to share."

"You did?"

"I used to be an assistant investigator in the New York District Attorney's office."

Bakso bent a knuckle. "Why'd you quit?"

"I tended to play too many lone hands, not always by the book."

Bakso grinned again. "It's as good a way as any to make yourself unpopular with the higher authorities. Well, it's been a pleasure to meet you — hope I've been helpful."

"Very."

"You staying on for a while?"

"Not long. I think I'll take a look at the bridge, though, before I go back to L.A."

"Day did it on the east side, not more'n seventy yards on."

"Thanks."

"You're welcome." Bakso extended a hard hand, then walked with me to the door. "I got to see the day captain about sump'n," he said.

I went out and waited on the sidewalk for a cruising taxi. The wait wasn't long and I was getting in when Bakso came out of the precinct station, turning left and walking fast.

The hackie said, "Where to, bud?"

I didn't answer immediately. I was watching Bakso. He turned into a coffee shop.

"Changed my mind," I said. I palmed the driver a dollar bill and started along the sidewalk. I had no clear notion why, except that Bakso had said he was seeing the captain of detectives — and manifestly wasn't.

The coffee shop was nearly full. I

stood for a moment on the threshold, looking. I could see the lieutenant crossing the floor diagonally, going towards a line of three pay telephone booths. He wedged himself in the middle one and dialled.

I went back on to the street, walking slowly. I was wondering why Lieutenant Bakso was using a pay telephone in a coffee shop instead of the one on his office desk.

3

I WALKED on to the Golden Gate Bridge. A blue sky and brilliant sunshine — but that wasn't going to last. In the distance mist was already seeping in from the ocean, recreating the precise conditions of Alvin Day's suicide leap. If it was suicide. Was the fog going to help? I didn't know, but it might suggest something.

Seventy yards on to the bridge, Basko had said. I paced out the distance, slowly and deliberately. Before I had completed the walk the mist was rolling right in. Suddenly, vision was partially blotted out. I stood for a moment, making sure of my bearings.

A figure loomed through the haze, coming towards me. A girl. I stopped again. The fog had moved further inland, engulfing me. By now the girl should have been almost level with me — but she wasn't.

I had an intuitive feeling that something was wrong. I went forward, fast and at an angle. The movement brought me close to the parapet. The girl was there, starting to climb. I closed in, making a long arm and jerking her back. She nearly fell against me.

"I wouldn't do it, if I were you," I said.

She half-turned to see me.

"Oh!" She gasped the exlamation.

"Come to think of it, I wouldn't do it if I wasn't you. That sounds crazy — but it's not half so crazy as what you were going to do."

"Leave me alone," she whispered. "Please leave me alone."

I still held her arm. "*Were* you going to jump off the bridge?"

"What difference does it make to you?" There was a tremor in her voice.

"*Were* you?"

She looked up at me, a pretty girl with a mass of fair hair framing her face. The blue eyes had a hunted look.

"Yes . . . " The word came out so low that I only just heard it.

I said gently: "You're too young to die. Not that it's a good idea at any age unless life has become totally insupportable."

"Mine has," she answered simply.

"You think it has, which isn't the same thing."

She didn't answer.

I said: "Look over the rail. You can't see the water because of the mist, but it's a two hundred and sixty-three foot drop and the impact will smash your body. Then the sharks will get it."

She shuddered violently.

"You don't really want that, do you?"

"I . . . I never thought of it like that. I just wanted out . . . everything seemed to have got on top of me . . . there seemed no point in going on living . . . " She paused, looking down at my hand.

34

"If I let you go will you promise something?" I said.

"Not to try again, you mean?"

"That, yes. Something else, though."

"What?"

"Will you have dinner with me?"

For the first time she made something close to a laugh. "You're not trying to pick me up, are you?"

"Not in the sense in which that remark is usually understood. I just figure you may be in need of a shoulder to cry on or lean on. Mine's available."

She laughed outright this time. It transformed the sombreness of her face. She looked at me again. Then she said: "I think you're a nice man."

"So you'll have dinner with me?"

"I don't know that I can eat after . . . " She didn't finish the sentence.

"We'll find the best restaurant they have in San Francisco and see if the menu tempts you. It'll tempt me," I added thoughtfully.

"You're funny," she said.

I released my grip. "Let's go . . . "

We walked slowly back along the bridge. After a moment she linked an arm in mine, not speaking. I said: "We ought to introduce ourselves, wouldn't you say?"

"I suppose we ought. I'm Judith Gresham. You can call me Judy."

"Dale Shand — and you can call me Dale."

"I'll do that. You probably saved my life just now."

"Probably?"

"Well, I don't know whether I'd have really done it."

"You were starting to climb the rails, Judy."

"Yes, I was — and I meant to jump off but I don't know whether I'd have found the courage at the last moment. Just the same, I was in a dangerous situation and you came along at the right time. I'm always going to be grateful."

We were off the bridge now. I flagged a taxi and said: "Drive us to the best

36

restaurant in town."

"There's more'n one competing for that title," the driver said.

I grinned. "Pick the one you'd choose if you were taking Sue-Ellen out to dine."

He looked at Judy. "She ain't her," he pointed out cleverly.

"No, but the idea's the same."

"In that case I'd take the lady to The Stardust. It'll cost you plenty," he added.

I winced slightly, as if an old wound was troubling me, but I said: "Drive us there."

The place was just off Park Presidio Boulevard at 14th Avenue. A nobly-appointed restaurant with, mercifully, no canned pop music, or any other kind of music. The Stardust was dedicated exclusively to the gastronomic arts. The gourmet in me silently approved.

I called for dry martinis and ordered the meal from a menu big enough for a small tablecloth. Then I sat back in my chair and said: "Now — why were you contemplating taking your own life?"

"The oldest story, what people used to call a shattered romance."

"Do you feel like talking about it, Judy?"

"Not to just anyone — but to you, yes. I owe you that much, don't I?"

"Sometimes it's easier to talk about intimate things to a stranger."

"Yes, it is."

"Maybe you should have done that before you went on to the bridge and met me."

"Perhaps. I couldn't bring myself to talk, though."

"You're talking to me."

She put out a slim hand and touched mine. "I said you *probably* saved me. It was more than probably. I really meant to jump, you know. If you hadn't stopped me I'd have . . . "

I said: "Would you like another martini while we're waiting?"

"I believe I would."

I signalled a roving bar waiter. The cocktails came and I said: "It'll help you to feel better."

"*You've* made me feel better. I don't know just how, but you have."

"And you won't ever try to do it again?"

"Never," she said.

"Nobody's worth it, you know. Life has to go on and you have to come to terms with it." I sipped the second martini, put the glass down and said directly: "Exactly what went wrong?"

"Everything was wrong — but I didn't know it until later. Not until after he walked out on me. I found out that he was already married. It took me some time to find out, from a friend of Bob's. Bob Stanton, that's his name. We met by chance on a cable car — it was before they decided to close the system and rebuild it — and got to talking and one thing led to another."

"You mean you slept with him?"

She coloured slightly. "Yes. I was in love, it wasn't just a casual relationship to me."

"But it was to Bob?"

She answered directly. "He said we'd get engaged. He had a small apartment downtown and I stayed there two nights. When I called the next day Bob wasn't there. I found that he'd sub-rented it for a month while the owner was away. Bob was in San Francisco on a business visit. His friend told me, a man named Bill Rush. He said Bob's home was in Dallas and that he'd gone back there . . . to his wife."

"I'm sorry." The words sounded mechanical.

She went on: "He didn't even leave a message. It turned out that he was just a skirt chaser. Bill said he'd had another girl before he met me. That was why he took an apartment instead of staying in a hotel . . . a place where he could lay a girl if he could find one." She coloured again. "He found me. Bill Rush said he'd tell any lie, even propose marriage, to get his way. The trouble was that I fell in love with him."

"Are you pregnant?"

"I was scared I might be and went to a doctor. He did some tests and said I didn't have to worry. That was a tremendous relief — but I was still shattered at what Bob had done to me, running out and not even leaving a farewell message. I thought of following him to Dallas. Bill gave me his address, but . . . "

"But you didn't?"

The waiter brought the starters, prawn cocktails, and she toyed with hers for a moment, then said: "If I confronted him all I'd achieve would be to hurt his wife."

"You're a nice girl, Judy," I said.

"I don't think of myself that way after sleeping with a married man."

"You didn't know he was married."

"No, he deceived me all ways."

"Do you hate him now?"

She shook her head. "I've fallen out of love but I don't hate him."

"I'm glad."

"Why?"

"If you hate it's a bad situation — hate can destroy you."

"I guess it can. I'm not very good at hating, anyway. In a sense I feel kind of sorry for him."

"A guy like that, he isn't worth the salt of your tears. Have you told your folks?"

"No. They live in Monterey. I haven't been home since Bob walked out on me."

"Why haven't you told your parents, Judy?"

"I didn't want to distress them. Also, I thought I ought to face it alone — try to come to terms with myself."

"You weren't succeeding very well if you were going to leap off the bridge, were you?"

"I didn't have that thought, not at first. Then, about three weeks ago, something happened that gave me the idea."

"What?"

"I was out walking, just aimlessly walking and thinking, when I found myself on the bridge. I didn't even remember going on to it. The sea mist came in, just like it did tonight, but I saw him."

"You saw who?"

"A man. He was near the parapet. Then the fog became dense and I couldn't see him. But I heard a cry and the other sound . . . "

"Like what?"

"It sounded like a body hitting the water. I ran forward to where I had last seen him — but there was nothing, he wasn't there. I thought he must have jumped. I ran back, looking for one of the bridge guards — but someone was already talking to them. He was shouting that he had seen this man jump."

"What did you do?"

"I thought that if they had a witness they didn't need me and I didn't want to get involved — I simply walked away in the fog. They hadn't seen me." She hesitated, then said in a low voice: "But I kept thinking about it and . . . "

I finished the sentence for her. "It gave you the same idea — started you thinking about going over the bridge yourself?"

"Yes, but it took me all of three weeks to nerve myself to go back on the bridge, almost exactly the same spot. Then . . . then you came along. I'm still not sure that I'd have found the courage to do it. But you settled it anyway, Dale."

I reflected slowly: "Three weeks, you said. Are you positive about the date?"

"I'm sure — why?"

"A man went over the bridge three weeks ago. His widow asked me to look into the circumstances. I haven't told you but I'm a private investigator visiting Los Angeles . . . "

"And now visiting San Francisco."

"That's right, though I normally work and live in England."

Her eyes widened. "In London?"

"Yes."

"You're an American, though you

44

have a sort of mid-Atlantic accent, haven't you?"

"I guess I have. I came over here on a three-week vacation. A lawyer I used to know asked me if I'd handle an inquiry for the widow and I agreed."

"The man who jumped off the bridge was from Los Angeles — I saw a piece in the paper about it. He must be the same man."

"His name was Alvin Day."

"That's right, I remember it now. Why does his wife want you to investigate it?"

"She thinks he was murdered. She doesn't have a shred of evidence but she says they were happily married and that he had no reason, financially or in any other way, to take his own life."

Judy stared. "You mean she thinks somebody *pushed* him off the bridge?"

I took my wallet out. "We'd better be quite sure we're talking about the same man." I extracted a polaroid snapshot colour print Larraine Day had given me. "Can you say if that's him?"

45

Judy Gresham peered down at it. "Yes — that's him. I only saw his features once before the fog rolled in but I think it's him."

"You saw him near the rails, but you didn't actually see him climb and jump?"

"No, because of the mist."

"But you got the impression that he might be going to do it?"

"I thought that, yes . . . " She paused, her forehead puckered. "Thinking back, I wasn't absolutely sure — but that's what I thought, so I ran towards him or where I had last seen him. Then I heard him cry out and there was a splash and I knew he had done it."

"He was alone?"

"I didn't see anyone with him . . . " She stopped, her eyes widening again. "You're not suggesting he *was* forced off the bridge!"

"I'm not suggesting anything, Judy — I'm just looking at every conceivable possibility."

"I didn't see anyone with him or

close by. But the fog had moved in, so I wouldn't. Someone *could* have moved in . . . "

I said slowly: "It's a long shot and maybe a wild one — but, unseen by you, someone *could* have pushed him over the rails and then simply walked away, in the other direction."

She thought for a moment, then said: "It's possible, I suppose."

"I'm not saying that's how it was, only that it *could* have been like that. But I've no proof. Incidentally, the man who called to the bridge guards was named Albert Fisher. He gave evidence at the coroner's inquiry."

"Yes, I remember seeing his name in the newspaper report. I'd forgotten until you mentioned it, then it came back." She paused again. "He said he saw the man jump off. I don't know how he could be so sure. I was closer and the fog prevented me from actually seeing him leap off."

"You're still sure about that?"

She nodded. "When I saw the

newspaper item I wondered if I ought to have gone to the police — but I thought it was too late. Also, by that time I was . . . "

"By that time you were contemplating going over the bridge yourself."

"Yes. I'm glad I didn't. I'm glad you came along."

"Apart from Alvin Day the only other persons on hand were you and Fisher?"

"That's right — well, apart from the other man."

I said sharply: "What other man? You haven't mentioned one before."

"I didn't think it mattered. It was when I was nearing the end of the bridge. He was walking in the same direction, just ahead of me. I thought he might have started walking on the bridge and then changed his mind and turned back on account of the mist."

"Or he could have seen pretty much what you saw and, like you, didn't want to get involved."

"I suppose he could. It didn't occur

to me. Do you think it might be important?"

"It depends on what he saw — specifically, if he happened to see more than you did."

"You'll have to ask him then."

"Are you saying you know him?"

"No, I don't know him, but I know where he can be found. He plays in a jazz group at a club called the Blue Note. I recognized him. He's a sax player — alto, tenor and baritone saxes. His name's Eddie Ryker. I've never spoken to him, but I know his name. I know the names of all the guys in the band because they're printed on a leaflet you get when you visit the place."

"You're a jazz fan?"

"I like the music — especially if it's Dixieland or Chicago style and that's the kind they play at the Blue Note."

I said: "You and me both."

By now we had finished the king salmon. Strawberries and ice cream arrived. I said meditatively: "I think

I'll drop by at the Blue Note. I take it you have to be a member to get in?"

"You can join on arrival — they'll be happy to sign you in."

"We could go together — if you don't mind the extended company of a man in early middle age."

"I like it," she said.

4

THE place was between Nob Hill and Portsmouth Square. They had a crescent-shaped sign out front which kept spelling *Blue Note Club*. The entrance was six steps down from the sidewalk, leading into a square foyer. A young fellow with thick brown hair and wearing, surprisingly, a conservative blue suit and matching tie, said: "Members or joining?"

Judy made a smile guaranteed to bring the roses to the most pallid cheek. "I'm a member, introducing a new member. My friend wishes to join — Mr Dale Shand."

"Happy to know you, Mr Shand. The membership fee is five dollars, plus five dollars entrance money."

I signed the register and parted with ten bucks.

The young fellow handed over a

membership card and turned to Judy. "Remember you now, you're Miss Judy Gresham. Haven't seen you in here for a week or two, maybe more."

Judy said: "Is the house band on?"

"Al Burke's Stompers, you mean?"

"That's right."

"They're just going on for their first set. The place isn't even half-full yet . . ."

Whatever he had been going to say was drowned by the din of the seven-piece outfit riding headlong into *Nobody's Sweetheart*. It sounded like pretty good Dixieland and I said as much.

"Tell that to Al and you'll have made a new friend," the blue-suited young fellow said.

We crossed the foyer into a wide, semi-basement room one of whose walls was covered with blown-up photographs of all-time jazz greats — Louis Armstrong, Jack Teagarden, Johnny Dodds, Bix Beiderbecke, Frankie Trumbauer, Benny Goodman, Sidney

Bechet, Earl Hines, Duke Ellington, Eddie Condon and Wild Bill Davidson. Most of them long gone, I mused sadly — though Wild Bill, that defiant cornet man from Defiance, Ohio, was still around and blowing up a jazz storm in his seventy-sixth year.

The floor was dotted with red-topped circular tables. I selected one near the stand. A few minutes later the band went into the coda, but almost immediately took off on *There'll Be Some Changes Made*, a torrid up tempo version reminiscent of the Condon mob in full cry.

I grinned. "They're delivering the authentic noise — I guess we'll have a drink to go with it." I got two Manhattans.

A girl with a pixie-like face came on, a small frail-looking girl. Not that there was anything frail about her singing voice. It soared across the dimly-lit room like a bomb:

Woke up this morning, somebody
  knocking on my door
Woke up this morning, somebody
  knocking on my door
It was my good man coming home
  once more . . .

I said: "That was really the blues.
She sounds like a cross between Trixie
Smith and Helen Humes — the best
qualities of each with a hefty piece of
herself added for good measure."

Judy laughed. "Tell her that and
you'll have made another new friend."

The group played three more numbers,
then took a short break, unannounced.

Judy said: "I don't see Eddie Ryker
on the stand."

"They had a guy on baritone, but
you mean he isn't Ryker?"

"No, I've never seen him before. He
must be new."

I waited for the band to come back,
then walked up to the stand. Al Burke,
who was manipulating the water key of
his trumpet, looked down inquiringly.

"You got a request we'll play it — if we know it, that is," he said with a grin.

"*After You've Gone* and the *Farewell Blues* would be swell, and permit me to say you have a great little band."

"After that you can call me Al."

"I'll do that. My name's Dale Shand — visiting from London and Los Angeles."

"I haven't seen you here before — this your first visit?"

"That's right, I came with Judy Gresham."

Burke, a stockily built fellow with thick ash-blond hair, glanced sideways. "Admire your taste," he offered.

"Thanks. It's a purely platonic relationship, though."

"Too bad . . . "

"I came to get an earful of good jazz — and something else."

"Yeah, what would that be?"

"I wanted to have a word with the sax player — not the one you're using right now. The regular one."

"You mean Eddie Ryker?"

I nodded.

"You know Eddie?"

"No, we haven't met. I wanted to talk to him about something. I heard that he played here nights."

"He did," Al Burke said shortly. Some of the amiability seemed to ebb from his broad face.

"The way you said that sounded like you were irritated about something, Al."

He hesitated, then went on: "Yeah, you can say that again. Eddie should've been here tonight. Instead, he sends a note round to my apartment saying he's quitting. I went round to his place to bawl him out, but he wasn't there. I had one hell of a job getting a dep in time for tonight."

"But you got one. He sounds okay."

"Yeah, Fred Hammerseld is one swell saxman. I was lucky to grab him."

I said: "Can you give me Eddie Ryker's address?"

"Why, is it important?"

"It may be."

He hesitated, but only briefly. "Apartment 7a, Gramercy Inn — it's in the sixteen hundred block,on Lincoln Avenue, near the Lincoln Park golf course."

I said levelly: "Mind if I look at the note, Al?"

Burke appeared to think for a moment. Then he said: "I guess there's no reason why not." He took a slip of notepaper from his inside breast-pocket.

What was on it was brief and decisive: *I've had an offer to join a band being formed for a place in Vegas, so I'm quitting as of now. Sorry there wasn't time to give notice. Best wishes. — Eddie Ryker.*

The writing had an odd look, as if the characters had been formed by someone unused to writing.

"Thanks for letting me see it, Al," I said.

"You're welcome. You can keep it if you want. If you meet up with him you can say he'd better not come back for his old job."

"I'll do that." I went back to the table and told Judy what the trumpet player had said.

"Do you think there's something significant in it?" she asked.

"Maybe — maybe not. The only way to find out is to see Eddie Ryker, if I can."

"You mean he may already be on his way to Vegas?"

"It's possible, in which case I may be wasting my time."

She eyed me thoughtfully. "But you're going to try, aren't you?"

"You read me accurately. I'll go after the band play a couple of requests for me. Will you stay on?"

"I think I will. I like it here and I'm feeling so much better, thanks to you. But we'll meet again, we must do. I'll give you my address." She wrote it on an envelope.

I gave her the name and telephone number of my hotel in Los Angeles.

"Are you coming back here later tonight, Dale?"

"Depends if I get through in time."

"The club stays open until two a.m. I'll still be here."

The band played the two numbers, finishing with a standout twelve-bar chorus on the blues. I leaned forward slightly and said: "I'll be in touch, Judy — that's a promise."

★ ★ ★

The Gramercy Inn belied its name. It wasn't so much an inn as a run-down apartment block which looked as if it hadn't been repainted since John F. Kennedy was President.

I stepped into a poorly illuminated reception area with a screen door over to the left bearing the legend, in chipped lettering: *S. P. J. Flugel, Propr.*

The door was marginally ajar. I palmed it wide open and went in. The Propr was sitting at an old-fashioned rolltop desk littered with what looked like an accumulation of invoices and receipts. As I entered his right hand made a fast dive into a deep drawer, but not so fast that I failed to see a half-empty gin bottle disappearing from view. A smeared glass stayed on the desk top.

Flugel said: "You want a room I got one, just one." He had a vaguely clogged voice, and moist eyes in a sharp greyish face. He was jacketless. He hooked fingers in red suspenders, snapping them up and down.

"I don't want a room," I said. "I'm calling on one of your tenants — a fellow named Ryker, Eddie Ryker."

"Oh, him?" Flugel leaned back in his chair, made as if to open the deep drawer, then took his hand away.

I said genially: "If you want a drink don't mind me."

"You saw me put the bottle away, huh?"

"You're entitled to take a drink on your own premises, Mr Flugel."

"That's right, I am. You care to join me?"

"Not right now."

"Suit yourself, Mr — what did you say your name was?"

"I didn't, but it's Shand. Is Eddie Ryker in?"

"He isn't and he won't be." The moist eyes flickered. "Does he owe *you* money?"

"No, it's nothing like that."

"Oh — I thought you might be a process server or a snatch-back man."

"Nothing like that, either. Why, does he owe you money?"

"To be honest, no. But he left kind of sudden."

"You mean he didn't give you notice?"

"Sure didn't." Flugel spilled gin into the smeared glass with a hand that was less than steady. "He left his rent, though, I got to admit that."

"And you don't happen to know where he's gone?"

"No — he left a note but it didn't

say. I got it here somewhere." Flugel rummaged among the clutter, found an envelope and said: "You can read it, if you like."

I took a folded sheet of paper from the envelope and read: *Enclosed please find rent in lieu of notice. I have to leave town for a new job which has come up unexpectedly. Yrs, E. Ryker.* The handwriting was oddly formed — like the writing on the note Al Burke had shown me.

"I take it he didn't say anything previously about getting another job?"

"No, he didn't. Not that we ever had much conversation." Flugel wiped his mouth with the back of his hand, added: "I didn't see much of him, if it comes to that. He never got up until around noon, sometimes later. He worked nights — a jazz musician."

I looked at the note again. A thought surfaced. "Did you ever see his handwriting before, Mr Flugel?"

"Once, yeah — just his signature when he took the apartment."

"Can you find it?"

"Why, what's it matter?"

I let a five-dollar bill flutter to the desk. "I'd appreciate seeing it," I said.

He picked up the five-spot, folded it twice and tucked it in his shirt pocket. "I guess that's a good enough entitlement, Mr Shand," he said cosily.

He stood up, crossed the small office to a faded olive green filing cabinet and came back with a folder from which he drew a tenancy agreement. The signature was at the bottom: E. Ryker and the date.

The writing bore no resemblance to that on the two notes I had seen. I still had the one Al had given me. I showed it.

Flugel peered down and said: "The writing ain't the same, is it?"

"So it seems."

"I don't get it," Flugel said. "Why should the writing be diff'rent?"

"I wish I knew."

"Kind of odd, isn't it?"

"Yeah, it is. And you don't have any

idea where he could be?"

"No way. I . . . " Flugel stopped.

I said: "Thought of something?"

"I just remembered. He has a sister. He mentioned it one time, one of the few times we ever got to talking. It was two-three months ago."

"Do you know where she lives?"

"He did say, yeah. Not sure I can recall the address. Wait a minute, though, while I think." Flugel's face puckered. Then he said: "I got it. He said she had an apartment over on Charles Street — near Half Moon Bay in South San Francisco. I don't know the number, though."

"Do you chance to know her name — her married name?"

"She ain't married. He said that. I remember it. Miss Adelaide Ryker. He called her Addy."

I let another five fall on the desk.

"What's that for?"

"You've earned it, Mr Flugel," I said.

64

5

IT was coming up to 10.30 p.m. Late to go calling on an unmarried lady you don't know — and without benefit of appointment. I went back to the hotel I had checked into for the night, found Miss Adelaide Ryker's number in the telephone book and called it.

"Yes, who is it?" The voice sounded a little nervous.

I said quietly, "The name is Dale Shand. We haven't met, but I was given your name. I understand you're Eddie Ryker's sister."

A pause, then: "That's right, I am. What do you want, Mr Shand?"

"I'd appreciate it if you would permit me to call on you, Miss Ryker."

"Well, I don't know, it's rather late . . ."

"I'm trying to contact your brother.

65

It occurred to me that you might be able to help."

"Oh . . . " She paused again.

"It could be important, Miss Ryker."

"He's not in trouble, is he?"

"Not that I'm aware of, Miss Ryker, but I'd like to talk with you, if I may."

"I've been worried about him, I haven't seen him in weeks."

"Perhaps we may be able to help each other, pooling what knowledge we have." I thought for a second and went on: "I'm a private investigator."

"Then Eddie *is* in some kind of trouble!" Her voice cracked on the words.

"I don't know of any trouble, Miss Ryker. I simply want to contact him about an inquiry I'm engaged on."

"Oh . . . well . . . I . . . "

"If you're worried about receiving me at this time of night call in a friend or neighbour."

"Can't we just talk over the telephone?"

"We can, but I have the feeling that it would be better if we met personally."

She said tentatively: "You *sound* genuine, Mr Shand."

"Eminently respectable is how I would phrase it, Miss Ryker."

She made a sound that was almost a small laugh. Then she said: "All right, you can call on me. Perhaps we *may* be able to help each other."

"We can try." I called reception and got them to order a taxi. It was waiting by the time I got to the entrance.

Charles Street was a quiet residential street of older-type houses and one-apartment blocks. I found the right apartment and poked a finger at the doorbell. The hall light came on, footsteps sounded and a voice called out: "Mr Shand?"

"Yeah."

The door opened on a thin woman with faintly angular features and mousy brown hair. She was wearing a crimson roll-top sweater and a pleated beige skirt and her small feet were in fleecy-lined house slippers.

"Please come in, Mr Shand . . . " She stopped and then said: "You *are* Mr Shand?"

"Dale Shand, the man who called you on the telephone."

She led the way into the living-room, turned and said with a quick smile: "I didn't call a neighbour in, I felt you were all right."

I made an answering smile. "Thanks for the implied compliment, Miss Ryker."

"I've fixed some coffee." She went into the kitchen and came back with a tray. "Why do you want to see Eddie?" she asked.

I said levelly: "Recently a man apparently leaped off the Golden Gate Bridge. I've reason to believe that your brother either saw him do it or saw him about to do it, just before the sea mist closed in. That's what I want to talk to him about."

"You mean it was a suicide?"

"The coroner decided that it was."

"And Eddie was a witness?"

"I think he may have been. I can't be sure. He didn't testify at the inquiry — another man was on the bridge and gave evidence."

"I'm not clear about this, Mr Shand. If it was suicide what's your interest?"

"The man who went over the bridge parapet was named Alvin Day. His home was in Pasadena. His widow asked me to investigate the circumstances."

"She isn't prepared to accept that it was suicide — is that it?"

I nodded. "That's how she looks at it, Miss Ryker."

"You can call me Addy," she said unexpectedly.

"I'll do that."

"Most everybody does." She poured coffee and went on: "If it wasn't suicide that leaves two alternatives, doesn't it?"

"Yeah."

"Accident . . . or murder," said Addy

Ryker calmly. "Which does she think it was?"

"The latter."

"Does she have any reason for thinking that, Mr Shand?"

"If I'm calling you Addy you'd better start calling me Dale. Answering your question, Mrs Day says they were happily married, lived quietly and that her husband had no money troubles or other problems."

"He could have them without his wife knowing, couldn't he?"

"He left her a substantial sum of money, so it couldn't be financial. As to other problems, I guess that's possible — but none seem to have emerged."

Addy Ryker said slowly: "She thinks someone pushed him off the bridge — and you think Eddie may have seen something which would bear that out?"

"You're moving too fast, Addy. I don't necessarily think that — I'm simply considering it."

"If Eddie saw anything suspicious he'd have gone to the police, wouldn't he?"

"He could have seen something, it could be no more than a glimpse, without connecting it with the death. He may not even have realized that Day went over the bridge."

"He'd see it in the newspaper . . ."

"Did *you* see it?"

"Well, no, I guess I didn't. But I don't read the papers much and Eddie always liked to."

"When I telephoned you said you had been worried about him and hadn't seen him in weeks."

"That's right."

"You don't think he's in trouble — or do you?"

She hesitated. "I don't know. He could be. Eddie's a bit wild times."

"In what way?"

"Liquor — and girls."

"It's not yet illegal. On the other hand, it could lead him into trouble."

"That's what I thought, especially

71

when he didn't come round to see me. He used to drop by at least once a week. Then he stopped coming and I started to feel anxious."

"Did you do anything about it?"

"I called his apartment several times. He said he'd been too busy to come round, but that everything was all right and I didn't have to worry."

"But you did?"

"Yes. I thought maybe he'd gotten involved with some woman, a married woman, and didn't come round in case I asked awkward questions. You see, I know Eddie's weaknesses."

"I take it he's a good deal younger than you, Addy?"

"Yes, he's pushing thirty-five and I'm fifty. Our parents died six years ago in a flu epidemic, within weeks of each other. They owned this apartment and left it to me. Eddie lived with me until about a year ago. We both came into some money. I invested mine. It wasn't a fortune, but it's useful. I mean it brings me a regular income. I work as well, though, as a telephonist. I guess Eddie's gone through his share by now."

"You know where he worked?"

"Not for sure — he played saxophone with various groups and never seemed to stay with one very long."

"Until recently he was with Al Burke's little band at a club called 'The Blue Note'. I went there tonight. Al said Eddie sent a note round saying he was quitting on account of he had a band job lined up in Las Vegas."

"Oh, I didn't know that."

"Al gave me Eddie's address and I went there. The guy who owns and runs the apartment house said Eddie left him a note, too, together with rent in lieu of notice."

"If Eddie's gone to Vegas what made you come here?"

"It was just possible that he might have told you something about his plans. Incidentally, the fellow at the apartment house knew where you lived. Eddie once told him."

"When you telephoned I mentioned that I hadn't seen him in weeks. I told you that."

"There was the chance that he might have told *you* over the telephone," I said, though this wasn't what I was thinking.

"Eddie didn't tell me anything about that — or anything else. All he said was that I didn't have to worry — and that was a while back. Do you think he's gone to Vegas?"

"I don't know. He could have. Or he could be staying with a friend before going there."

"Knowing Eddie, he could be shacked-up with some girl," his sister said.

I tried another angle. "Apart from being a professional musician did he have any other kind of work or . . . " I stopped. "Have you thought of something?"

"It was what you just said, it made me remember. He rented a small lock-up shop on North Franklin Street selling musical instruments by day and working in the band nights."

I wondered why Al Burke hadn't said anything about Eddie running a shop. Maybe he simply thought Eddie would have closed the place anyway if he was going to Vegas.

Addy said: "It was only a small business, just part-time. I don't think he made much money out of it. It was only open from around midday to six in the evening — he wasn't one for getting up early."

"The fellow who owns the apartment house said he often didn't get up until midday."

"If you find him will you let me know?"

"That's a promise, Addy." I stood up. There was a framed photograph on the overmantel. It showed a smooth-faced young fellow wearing a tuxedo and holding an E-flat alto saxophone.

"That's Eddie — the picture was taken three years ago when he was still living here."

A thought started in my mind. "Did

Eddie ever write to you?"

"Only once. It's in the desk." She got the letter out. "You can read it if you like."

It was a brief letter and what was in it wasn't important. But the handwriting was — it bore no resemblance to the writing on the two notes Al Burke and Flugel had received.

I handed back the letter and said: "Thanks for letting me call, Addy. I'm grateful."

She gave me her hand. "When you catch up with Eddie please tell him to call me."

"I will, but if he's gone to Vegas it may take a little time before I find him."

"Tell him to come and see me as soon as he's able. And I hope you'll come and see me again yourself," she added.

It was too late to go calling on a small lock-up shop. Or was it? I got a taxi to North Franklin Street. There was just the chance that he might be there. If he was, it would save me going to Vegas.

The street was near the waterfront, a short street of walk-up apartments and a handful of small shops. I found the one I was looking for — a single-storey lockup with a window screening guitars, trumpets, saxes and a drum kit. Over the window was a sign: *Eddie Ryker, Band Instruments*.

The door was locked — well, I hadn't expected to find it open. Maybe he was already in Vegas. But he might have left a clue like a Vegas address, a scribbled note — anything. My mind made itself up. I took a slim section of celluloid from my wallet and used it to manipulate the wards of the lock. They slid back, but the door didn't open. That meant it was bolted on the inside. I could feel myself stiffening. If the bolt had been shot it could mean that Eddie was still on the premises . . . unless he had gone out the back way.

There was no passage down the side of the store, but there had to be one somewhere. I walked a little way along the street until I found it. The darkness there was almost opaque, but I navigated my way down it, came out on a narrow dirt lane and counted my way back to the rear of the shop.

The rear door had a frosted glass panel let into it. It also had an old-fashioned trigger handle. I depressed it and pushed, not hard. It wasn't necessary. The door opened inwards. I got my gun out, a Colt automatic, nine-shot. I freed the safety catch and stepped into what appeared to be a store-room; I could dimly make out several packing crates.

I reached up the side of the wall, found a switch and thumbed it down. Lights came on in the room but nobody challenged me. Maybe Eddie Ryker had gone out leaving the door on the latch. Yeah, maybe Christmas comes on Midsummer's Day.

A musty corridor led from the store-room to the front of the shop. I got more lights on and trod carefully along it. There was another door to the front of the premises. As I neared it my nostrils twitched, catching the hang-over of spent cordite. I kicked the door wide open and went in.

Eddie Ryker was lying sideways in a dark corner of the floor with his left leg buckled under him. There was a blackened hole in the front of his white shirt, on the left side. Not much blood because it had been a contact wound. I reached down and probed the big neck artery, but it wasn't strictly necessary because I knew I was looking at the late Eddie Ryker.

6

HE hadn't been dead long. The whiff of cordite proved that, and *rigor mortis* hadn't set in.

I went methodically through his pockets. A cheap ballpoint pen, a gas cigarette lighter, a small comb, some coin money and an envelope containing an airline ticket to Las Vegas. No billfold, though there must have been one. Its absence suggested a robbery motive — but it could have been calculated to suggest exactly that.

A drawer in the back of the counter contained a stack of invoices and receipts, some correspondence from a firm of instrument suppliers and a small stiff-backed book in which sales had been noted. Nothing else.

Meanwhile, there was a dead man lying on the floor. I turned the body slightly, enough to see that the bullet must have gone right through. I found it in a corner near the counter flap. Leaving it there had been a mistake because a gun can be identified by the rifling on the slug — except that first you have to find the gun. Just the same, it was a mistake; unless the killer had had to fade in a hurry.

Either way, the law would have to be told. I toyed with the idea of calling Central Homicide and merely saying: 'There's a dead man in Eddie Ryker's music shop at 4789 North Franklin — the coroner will want to know' and then hanging up.

Reluctantly, I decided against it. Instead, I made the call and said: "Put me through to the captain of detectives."

A flat voice sounded in my ear. "Wuddia want?"

"I've just found a man shot dead. The captain of detectives should be informed."

"Hold on!"

Seconds later another voice came down the wire. "Captain Halls speaking. Who are you and where are you?"

"Shand is the name, Dale Shand. I'm visiting San Francisco from L.A. I'm at 4789 North Franklin — Eddie Ryker, Band Instruments, a small lock-up shop. I called there in the hope of seeing Ryker and found him lying on the floor, shot dead through the heart at point-blank range. He hasn't been dead long."

"You're sure he's dead?"

"Quite sure, Captain."

"We'll be there in minutes, Mr Shand. Stay right by the body. Don't move it, don't touch anything. Understood?"

"Understood."

Halls put the receiver down. I lifted the counter flap again and unbolted the front door. It was on the lock but not double-locked. It could be opened by pulling back a trigger. I pulled it back, leaving the door ajar.

I tamped flake tobacco down in my pipe and sat there smoking it, but not for long. In slightly less than five minutes sirens wailed out on the dark street, heavy footsteps sounded and Captain Halls strode in, followed by a fellow I took to be a detective lieutenant, also a detective sergeant and two bluecoats, one with a camera. Behind them came the ambulance crew.

Halls was a large blond man around fifty years old with keen blue eyes in a slightly craggy face. He was wearing a medium grey suit of stylish cut. His thick hair had a stylish cut, too.

"Mr Shand?" Without waiting for a reply he went on: "Bernard Halls, captain of detectives, Homicide. With Detective Lieutenant Nick Hobart and Detective Sergeant Hymie Roper." He didn't introduce the two harness bulls.

Nick Hobart said: "Where's the stiff?"

"The body's where I found it, Lieutenant." I nodded in the direction.

They went across the floor. Hobart, down on one knee, said tersely: "The guy's a dead pigeon all right. You a friend of his?"

"No, I never saw him before."

Hobart stared. "How d'you come to be here, then?"

"I'll explain while your men are taking pictures and chalking the floor," I said patiently.

"We're here to listen — among other things," Halls said. "You mentioned on the telephone that you were from Los Angeles."

"That's right, though I normally live in London, England. I'm a private investigator."

Hobart's face went a little tight. "What's a gumshoe out of London and L.A. doing in San Francisco?" His voice suddenly sounded hostile.

"Let him tell it, Nick," said Halls impassively.

I went on: "I'm in San Francisco acting for a Mrs Larraine Day, of Pasadena, whose husband, Alvin Day, died in a fall from the Golden Gate Bridge."

Halls palmed a hand along the side of his hair. "I remember it, though it wasn't a homicide case. Just another suicide off the bridge. Detective Lieutenant Bakso handled it, in case there *was* foul play. What did the widow want you to do?"

"She wasn't willing to accept that her husband killed himself and asked her lawyer if he could recommend a private investigator. The lawyer's name is Charles Forbes. We used to be friends years ago in New York. I'm over here on holiday and made a point of calling on Forbes. He asked me if I would see Mrs Day. I did."

"A private eye from Los Angeles don't have any official standing here," Hobart said.

"Forbes fixed temporary cover in L.A. and San Francisco — he's friendly with the D.A. in both cities. I called on Lieutenant Bakso and explained why I was here. He was apparently satisfied that it was a suicide case and figured that Mrs Day was letting her imagination run away with her."

Nick Hobart seemed about to say something, but Halls cut in. "Go on," he said quietly.

"After I left Lieutenant Bakso I went out on to the bridge to take a look at the exact spot where Alvin Day went over. I didn't expect to find anything, it was just to see the spot. While I was there I got into conversation with a young lady, a Miss Judy Gresham. It turned out that she was on the bridge the evening Day fell — or jumped. She saw him approaching the side, then the mist hid him from view."

Hobart sniffed. "Nothing in that, then."

"You haven't put it in as many words, but I'm taking it that Mrs Day thinks her husband was pushed off the bridge — murdered?" Halls said.

"Yeah."

"What do *you* think, Mr Shand?"

"I'm keeping an open mind, Captain."

"What else did this Miss Gresham tell you?"

"She mentioned that a man alerted the bridge guards. I guess that would be the man named Albert Fisher who gave evidence at the coroner's inquiry."

"How do you come to know that?"

"Lieutenant Bakso told me — apparently Fisher's testimony backed up the suicide theory."

Halls nodded. "Yes, though it doesn't explain if and how this man Ryker comes into it."

"Miss Gresham told me that as she left the bridge she saw Ryker . . . "

"You mean she knew him?"

"Not personally, but she knew who he was. Eddie Ryker is or was a jazz musician working in a group at the Blue Note Club. She had visited the place and recognized him."

"Did she think Ryker saw something?"

"She simply recalled that he was on the bridge at the time Day fell. I thought it might be worth while talking to him. I went with her to the club and Al Burke, the band leader, told me Ryker had quit apparently to take a band job in Las Vegas. He gave me Ryker's address — an apartment at a place called the Gramercy Inn — but he had checked out. The guy who owns and manages the apartments said Ryker had a sister, a Miss Adelaide Ryker. I called on her tonight in the hope that she might know where her brother was in Vegas. She didn't — but she said he had a small musical instruments business on North Franklin. I came here on the off-chance and found him dead."

Halls said: "How did you know it was him?"

"Miss Ryker showed me a photograph of him."

"I see. How did you get in?"

"The street door was locked and bolted. I went round the back."

"Why?"

"I thought that if I got in there might be a chance of finding an address in Vegas."

"Sounds like unlawful entry, if not a break-in," said Hobart.

"No break-in, Lieutenant. The rear door was on the latch."

Hobart sneered. "You had no legal right to walk in, pal."

"Strictly speaking, no — but maybe it's as well that I did, otherwise the body could have remained here indefinitely, without anyone knowing."

Halls said: "I'll give you that, Mr Shand, and because of it I'm going to pass up the question of unlawful entry. Just what did you expect to get from this man Ryker?"

"I don't know that I actually expected anything, Captain. There was just the chance that he did see more than the others that night on the bridge. I didn't think it was much of a chance, but it seemed worth finding out."

"Like if Ryker saw someone push Day over the bridge rails?

"I'm not saying that was how it was, but it's a possibility."

"If he saw or thought he saw anything like that he'd have come to us, wouldn't he?"

"He *should* have done."

"What's that supposed to mean?" demanded Hobart.

"I'm looking at the possibility that he didn't want to get involved."

Halls grinned wryly. "It's been known," he said.

One of the ambulancemen said: "Everything's been marked out. Okay we remove the body, Captain?"

Halls nodded.

I watched them put the body on a stretcher. When they had gone I said slowly: "I had no particular theory about where Eddie Ryker fitted in — I simply wanted to talk with him. But the fact that somebody shot him dead could be the start of a reopening of the case, couldn't it?"

"Yeah, though it doesn't necessarily have a bearing on the Alvin Day business."

"It's a coincidence, though, and I don't like coincidences — more especially in a murder case."

"That makes two of us."

"On the other hand, Lieutenant Bakso seemed to be fully satisfied that Day took his own life."

"Yeah."

"I take it you'll be seeing him about the Ryker angle, Captain?"

Halls stared. "Didn't he tell you?"

"Tell me what?"

"That he was on his last day in the service."

"No, he didn't say that. You mean he resigned and today was his final duty detail?"

"Yeah. He put in his resignation around the time of the Day affair. The notice period expired this afternoon."

"He didn't mention that to me and we had quite a chat."

"Well, he probably didn't think it necessary. So far as he was concerned the case had been finalized." Halls pondered for a moment, then said quietly: "There isn't anything to suggest that this shooting connects in any way with Alvin Day . . . or do you think there could be?"

I spread both arms in a gesture. "I don't have any evidence of that, Captain."

"A theory perhaps?"

"All I wanted was a talk with Eddie Ryker."

"In case he did see something — something which he decided, for whatever reason, to keep to himself?"

Before I could answer Hobart said: "The guy could of been linked with one of the mobs and got outa line."

"It's possible — the way anything is possible, I guess."

"We'll see what we can turn up," Halls observed. "You'll have to take the stand when the coroner opens his inquiry. That'll be tomorrow."

"I can return to Los Angeles afterwards, I take it?"

"No problem. The only testimony the coroner will require from you will be evidence of finding the body. Incidentally, Bakso resigned to go and live in L.A. We understand he's taking up a security job there.

As a matter of fact, he left for Los Angeles tonight."

"I might run across him then."

"He said a finance house had made him an offer which was too good to pass up, but he didn't give a name," Halls said indifferently.

I thought it was odd that Bakso hadn't mentioned that he was on his last day with the San Francisco police. Like it was odd that he used a pay telephone booth when he could have made the call from the precinct station. But I kept both thoughts to myself — also the fact that the writing on Eddie Ryker's two notes wasn't the same as in the letter Addy had shown me. More like a right-handed man using his left hand. Why should Ryker do that? Maybe he didn't . . .

Halls said: "The bullet went right through Ryker — we'd better look for it."

I speared an index finger. "It's over there. I didn't pick it up."

"Or touch it?"

"No, I left it for you."

Hobart picked it up in a folded handkerchief tissue. "It's a .38 calibre, Captain." He laughed shortly. "All we got to do is find the gun it was fired from. Like looking for a needle in a haystack."

"We can try," Halls said phlegmatically.

★ ★ ★

I got back to the Blue Note Club at 1.45 a.m. Judy Gresham said: "I thought you weren't coming."

"I promised I'd make it if I could, Judy."

"Did you see Eddie?"

"I found him at a small musical instruments shop he owns . . . or owned."

"I don't quite follow that," she said.

I had to tell her. "He was lying on the shop floor — somebody had shot him dead."

Judy made a small shocked sound.

"I called the police. I've had quite

a session with them. It's a murder one rap. I'll have to testify at the coroner's inquiry tomorrow . . . well, today now."

"But how . . . I mean why would anybody kill him?"

"I don't know, but I have a feeling that it links in some way with the Alvin Day case. I don't know how, but I think it does."

She made a small shiver. "What a dreadful thing — he seemed a nice guy."

"Nice guys can get killed, Judy."

"I suppose so. But what a dreadful thing," she said again.

"Would you like a drink?"

"Yes, I think so. I haven't had one since you left."

"I'll get two brandies."

A waiter brought them. She drank some of hers, not speaking. She still looked shocked.

I said: "I'll see you home. It's not safe for a lone girl to be out at this hour — or maybe any other hour."

"I'll be all right, I've ordered a taxi for two o'clock."

"Just the same I'll see you home."

She had a bachelor apartment in a modern block on Laxby Street. She keyed the lock, half turned and said: "Come in for a few minutes, Dale."

I followed her into a living-room furnished with feminine taste.

"Shall I fix some coffee?"

I looked at her. "You're tired and shocked. Old Doctor Shand recommends sleep."

"I *am* a little tired . . . but it's the other thing that's in my mind. Will I be seeing you again?"

"Soon, I hope."

"You'll telephone me after you get back to Los Angeles?"

"Unless forcibly restrained."

That made her laugh, banishing some of the tension. She came closer, putting her cheek up for a kiss. I wanted to take her in my arms, holding her soft warm body against mine.

Instead, I said: "Goodnight, Judy

— I'll be seeing you."

I went out without looking back.

* * *

At eleven o'clock the next morning I gave formal evidence of finding the body. The police didn't press the point about the way I let myself into Eddie Ryker's shop.

I lunched in the hotel, checked out and called a taxi.

I was waiting on the sidewalk when a parked Mercury started up, screeched forward and mounted the kerb, coming straight for me. With no more than a split second to spare I jumped backwards. The car swung back into the roadway, shot forward on an upward surge of gear shifts and vanished in the traffic driven by a man with a black beard, huge rounded sunglasses and a Panama hat. He could be anybody.

An elderly passer-by said: "Are you all right, sir?"

"Yeah, I'm all right."

97

"You jumped back just in time. The way some people drive these days . . . " The elderly party made a clicking sound with his tongue. "You could have been killed, sir."

Maybe that was the idea, I said — but not audibly.

7

IT was coming up to 6 p.m. when I got back to Los Angeles. I used an airport telephone to call Alvin Day's office.

A baritone voice said: "George Lane speaking — who is calling?"

"Dale Shand, acting for Mrs Larraine Day."

"Mrs Day telephoned me yesterday afternoon, Mr Shand. I gathered you were going to San Francisco."

"I've been and come back, Mr Lane. I'd like to meet you."

"I was about to close the office for the rest of the day, but I can delay that if you want to come right away."

"If it doesn't inconvenience you, Mr Lane."

"Or even if it does, eh?"

"Let's just say that I'd welcome the opportunity of seeing you."

"I'll wait. Where are you speaking from?"

"The airport. I'll be with you shortly."

I collected my rented car from the airport parking lot and drove there. The late Alvin Day's offices were in a small block of business premises. I put the car on the forecourt and went in.

I had subconsciously expected to find that Lane was a stooped elderly man; instead, he turned out to be a tall athletic young fellow in his thirties with a tanned face.

He held out a strong hand, motioned me to a seat and said: "What can I do for you, Mr Shand?"

"I'm not sure that you can do anything, Mr Lane, but I judged it desirable to call. I understand from Mrs Day that her husband's affairs are in good order."

"They are — Mr Day was an exceptionally meticulous man."

"Mrs Day told me her husband left her well provided for, so the business must have been prosperous."

"It was and is. He once told me he had something of a struggle getting established, but that was years ago."

"It seems a pity to have to wind it up," I suggested.

Lane fingered the plain gold links on his shirt cuff, then said: "I've discussed that with Mrs Day — this morning, as a matter of fact. The upshot is that she has decided to continue the business, in association with myself as manager and chief executive."

"As the business is profitable that sounds like a sensible move."

"Yes. It's also good for me," Lane admitted candidly. "I don't have enough capital to buy. Then Mrs Day suggested I should run it for her. I'm extremely grateful."

"Does she intend playing an active part?"

"Fairly active — as president. She will have the final say on all decisions and policy matters but will leave the day-to-day running to me."

"It sounds like an admirable arrangement — both for Mrs Day and yourself."

"That's so. It gives Mrs Day a new interest in life — and promotes me to executive status at a considerable financial gain. Mrs Day is being generous in the matter of salary and, in addition, I am to have a percentage share in the net profits."

"You're candid, Mr Lane, and I like that."

Lane grinned quickly. "You'd probably have found out anyway."

"It's possible, but the point is that you told me yourself. I'll be no less frank and tell you what happened in San Francisco on my trip there."

Lane listened without interruption. Then he said slowly: "It *could* be murder then."

"It's looking like that. Right now I'll go so far as to say there is something wrong about the entire set-up."

"For a start I'd guess that there's something odd about this cop Bakso.

102

Specifically, that he knows more than he's told."

"I go along with that, though it doesn't necessarily follow that he had anything to do with Day going off the bridge."

"Do you figure he knew this man who was shot?"

"He may have done, though there's nothing to back up that theory."

"If Ryker was on the bridge at the relevant time he has to fit in somewhere," Lane said. He went on: "The guy you think drove his car at you also fits in somewhere. You never saw him before?"

"No. Mind you, with a Panama hat, sunglasses and a heavy beard he must have been in disguise."

"I suppose so. I . . . " Lane paused, as if uncertain how to proceed.

"If you've just thought of something, Mr Lane, I'd like to hear what it is."

His mouth twitched faintly. "You don't miss out on anything, do you?"

"*Is* there something?"

For a long moment he was silent. Finally, he said, as if with reluctance: "There *is* something else, yes. I don't know whether it has any bearing on your inquiries for Mrs Day — and, in any event, I wouldn't like it to be passed on to her."

"I can't promise not to tell her if circumstances appear to make it necessary — but I'll try to respect whatever confidence you're about to repose in me, Mr Lane."

"It may have no connection with your case."

"You'd better let me be the judge of that." I took out my pipe. "Do you mind if I smoke?"

"I don't smoke myself — but go ahead. I'm not the kind of non-smoker who wants to stop everybody else."

"I appreciate that."

George Lane sat very straight in his chair. "Did Larraine tell you anything about their married life?"

"She said they were happily married

and lived very quietly and that with rare exceptions her husband always came home on time."

"That's right, he did. There were occasions when he was out of town on a business trip, but the occasions were rare." Lane started fidgeting with his gold cuff-links again, then said almost in a rush: "Just the same, he was seeing a woman."

I took the pipe from my mouth and said: "How do you know that?"

"I saw them together in his car," replied Lane simply.

"When was this?"

"Six-seven weeks ago. I had a business call to make and came back through Glendale. I made a detour off the main highway to avoid the traffic. I saw Alvin's car parked under a tree. She was in the car with him."

"Maybe she was a client."

"I'd have thought that but for one thing — they were embracing."

"You're sure?"

Lane said: "They were in a clinch, kissing."

"What did you do?"

"I just drove straight past. They didn't see me. They were very much otherwise engaged."

"The woman — did you know her?"

"No. Incidentally, she was a young woman, a stunning blonde with very long hair. I saw that much as I went by."

"I'm taking it that you didn't say anything to Day?"

"It wasn't any of my business, even though I was on friendly terms with both Alvin and Larraine. But that's not all."

I waited.

Lane hesitated again, then said: "I remembered later that he had been absent from the office on a number of occasions — always in the afternoon. He said he had been seeing clients, but he didn't say who they were. In the light of what I chanced to see I concluded that he had been keeping clandestine appointments with the blonde girl. Well, he must have, mustn't he?"

"Or with more than one."

Lane looked startled. "I hadn't thought of that."

"I was being a little facetious. As of now we'd better settle for one at a time. You never saw her before, so you won't have any idea who she is?"

"No — why, do you want to talk to her?"

"It might disclose more of Day's private background — the part of his life that he apparently succeeded in keeping from his wife."

"You don't think it links with his death in any way, do you?"

"I don't know. I'd like to follow it up. Did he have any men friends?"

"He never went around with one, at least not to my knowledge . . . wait a minute, though, he did have a talk in the office some time back with Ted Lally."

"You mean someone who wasn't a client?"

"Well, Lally *may* have been seeing Alvin professionally, but I doubt it."

"Why?"

"Ted Lally inherited a chain of luxury apartments some years ago and sold out at a very fat price. Since then he's spent his time acquiring something of a reputation as a playboy. It could be that . . . " Lane moved his shoulders in a gesture.

"You're thinking that he may have introduced Day to this girl?"

"Well, I don't know, but I'd say it's possible . . . In fact, more than possible — because we never did any realty business with Lally, I know that."

"Thanks for telling me. I'll pay him a call — I can find his address in the telephone book."

"I can save you that small trouble. He lives at a house called Four Winds on Lasalle Street just off West Adams Boulevard near the big house Fatty Arbuckle bought at the height of his fame, before the Virginia Rapp scandal."

"You're peeping back into the distant past, Mr Lane."

"Yeah, before my time. Before yours, too."

I drove to West Adams and found the house — a handsome single-storey house with a snow trim and a cool green roof set back from the roadway and hidden from it by a line of carefully tended trees. The ornamental wrought-iron gates were open and a flagged driveway curled round a smooth green lawn which looked as if it had just come from the cleaners.

I tramped up three wide concrete steps and leaned my weight on a bell rope. After a moment the door was opened by a thickly-built man in his fifties with glittering black eyes and an eagle's beak for a nose. He was wearing what appeared to be the tribal uniform of the Brigade of Butlers.

"Yes, sir?" The voice was a rolling *basso-profundo* with the inflexions of old Italy. Or Sicily. Most likely the latter.

I said who I was, adding: "I'd appreciate seeing Mr Ted Lally, if he's in."

The glittering eyes surveyed me for a moment. Then: "The master is in, Signor Shand. Whether he will consent to see you is a matter for him to decide, eh?"

I beamed. "Start getting it decided, *amico*."

The butler did not actually smile, but a small muscular spasm on his face suggested that he was on the verge of it. He held the door wide open and intoned: "Please to take a seat in the hallway, sir."

I took one. The butler went away. He was back in a few seconds, announcing: "Please to follow me, *si*."

He marched down the hallway, a dignified procession of one, and into a room which looked as if it could seat a dozen people in spacious comfort. Standing in the middle of it in splendid isolation was a tall man with a slightly corrugated face topped by waving dark brown hair flecked with grey. He was wearing not less than nine hundred dollars worth of exquisite tailoring and moved forward with a sort of languid grace which could be natural or not.

He organized a long smile against perfect white teeth which could also be natural or not and said: "In what way can I brighten your life, Mr Shand?"

"You may be in a position to give me a small piece of information."

"Offhand, I can't think of anything I know that would interest a private eye." He promoted the recent smile into a laugh. "Come to think of it, on the other hand I might. Would you care for a drink?"

"If you're having one I'll join you."

"I'm always having one." He crossed the room to a cocktail bar angled in a corner. "Scotch on the rocks then." He fixed the drinks, perched himself on a tall bar stool and said briefly: "Shoot."

"I've been engaged by a Mrs Larraine Day to look into the circumstances surrounding the death of her husband, Alvin Day. I gather from another source that you knew him."

"Slightly. He wasn't a close friend." Lally picked up his glass, not yet drinking from it. "Is there some special thought behind this?"

I didn't answer directly. Instead, I said: "I take it you are aware that Alvin Day apparently jumped to his death off the Golden Gate Bridge in San Francisco?"

Lally's face hardened slightly. "Read it in the newspapers," he said shortly. He drank some of his drink, put the glass down and went on: "I can't imagine what this has to do with me. Incidentally, Day didn't apparently jump off the bridge — he jumped."

"His widow thinks he was pushed off."

Lally stared. "You mean murdered?"

"That's what I'm trying to find out."

"I thought the coroner and the police

112

were satisfied that it was suicide."

"They were, but they could be wrong."

"I see. Or, rather, I don't quite see. But either way, I certainly don't connect with it."

"I'm not suggesting it. I'm simply contacting people who knew Day in the hope that somewhere along the line I'll get a lead. Your name was given to me by George Lane."

"I don't know a George Lane."

"Lane was employed by Day in a managerial capacity. Mrs Day has decided to continue the business with Lane as chief executive. Lane says you called in to see Day some time ago. He didn't know you personally, but he knew about you."

Ted Lally grinned. "Freely translated, I guess that means he knew me by reputation."

"I gathered that. He said you have a reputation as a playboy."

"I like the good things of life — good food, good liquor and not-so-good women. So what?"

"Lane saw Day in a parked car with a girl he describes as a stunning blonde. As they were embracing he figured that Day was having an affair with her. Lane didn't know her but he thought you might."

For a few seconds Lally stayed silent. Then he said: "Look here, Alvin had a happy marriage. I don't want to say anything that would get back to Larraine Day."

"It won't — unless circumstances make it inescapable. You have my word on that, Mr Lally. As a start do you mind telling me how you came to know Day?"

"We both happened to be staying at the same hotel in San Diego. I was on a private visit. Day was staying overnight in connection with his business, I understood. We got to talking in the bar. Well, you know how it is — one thing led to another and the subject of women got into the conversation."

Lally lit a cigarette and went on

levelly: "If you want it straight, he was looking for a girl. Not any stray hooker, but a girl with looks and style who would give him a time and maintain total discretion about it. We got quite friendly, the way you do over a few drinks. The upshot was that we arranged to meet a few nights later in the Gilded Slipper Club off Wilshire Boulevard."

"Larraine Day told me he was rarely absent from home nights."

"Yeah, Alvin told me the same thing. This must've been one of the rare occasions."

"What exactly took place when you went to this club?"

"I introduced him to a blonde I know — Mitzi Bellson. She sings the odd number with the small band they have there — not professionally, they just let her do it. As a matter of fact, she's no slouch as a singer and could probably do well if she took it up seriously. But I guess she pulls down plenty being agreeable to the well-heeled heels who go there — me included. Anyway, Alvin fancied screwing her and she was willing."

Lally grinned again. "On account of his home life Mitzi had to accommodate him afternoons only — matinée performances, you might say. I called in at his office one day just for a chat — that would be when Lane saw me."

I nodded. "It was at the time he had started wondering about Day's unexplained absences in the afternoons."

"And when he saw me in the office he put two and two together and got the sum right — knowing my reputation?"

"That's about it."

"And now you want to question Mitzi?"

"She may know something, even without realizing it."

"Such as?"

"Something more about Day's background. In particular, whether he had

116

made an enemy or enemies. Perhaps some seemingly small thing which could put the whole case in a different perspective."

"He didn't say anything to me about having made enemies, but he probably wouldn't. If he *was* thrown off the bridge there must be one, I guess."

"If his wife's theory is right there has to be one."

"Yes." Lally moved on the stool. "Would you care for another drink?"

"Why not?"

"Splendid!" Lally made two more and said slowly: "If you're seeing Mitzi you can mention my name, if you have to."

"Meanwhile, it would help if you described her to me."

"She's one swell looker. Between twenty-five and thirty, a tall blonde with the figure of a show girl. Oval face, wide mouth and green eyes with amber flecks. She has a small white scar on her left hip, if you get that far with her."

"I wasn't proposing to try," I said austerely.

"You might change your mind when you see her. She can be very cooperative. In bed I mean." He ran a finger down the side of his face. "I've just remembered. I've a picture of her. Hold on while I get it." He went from the room and came back with a snapshot colour print taken close up. It showed a striking-looking girl with a bold expression on her face. I thought she was more likely to be in her early thirties than her middle or late twenties.

"I guess I'll know her on sight," I said.

"Yeah, she's easy to remember, as Bing Crosby used to sing." Lally put out a hand. "Well, good luck — and happy to have been of service to you, Shand."

"It's appreciated," I said and started down the hallway preceded by the butler, who had materialized apparently from nowhere in particular. I drove to my hotel and was going into my suite when the telephone rang. A remembered voice came over the line.

"Dale — is that you?"

"Yes, it's me. Hello Judy."

"I thought I might catch you at this time."

"I'm glad you did — it's nice to hear your voice again. What can I do for you?"

"Nothing, but I may be able to do something for you. I ran into Al Burke at lunchtime. He said he's remembered something about Eddie and I thought maybe I should tell you."

"Go on Judy."

"He said Eddie was friendly with a man named Art Jones who lives in an apartment on Carling Street. Al called there to see if he could get Eddie's address in Vegas. I told him about Eddie being shot. There was a piece about it in the papers but Al hadn't read it."

"Did he get an address?"

"No, and that's the odd part of it — Art Jones wasn't at his apartment and a neighbour said he hadn't been seen around for some little time." Judy paused, then went on: "I don't know if it matters, but I thought you might like to know."

"There may be a connection, Judy."

"With Eddie dead and Art Jones missing it looks as if . . . " She left the rest of the sentence unfinished.

I completed it. "It looks as if Art Jones could have killed Eddie, you mean?"

"Well, I don't know, but . . . "

"It's a possibility — but not a certainty. For one thing, he seems to have quit his apartment some time ago."

"He could have taken another one — people change their apartments. I mean it's funny he should be missing at this particular time."

"Yes, it is."

"Do you think I ought to go to the police?" She hesitated. "I don't really want to, but I will if you think I should."

"I'll call them, Judy. I know Bernard Halls, the captain of detectives. I'll put him on to Al Burke. The thing may be a coincidence, but Halls had better be informed."

"Of course, Art Jones may merely have left San Francisco on business."

"Maybe, maybe not. Halls will find out one way or the other. There may not be a connection — but somebody had better find out, or try to. How are you, Judy?"

"I'm fine."

"Not depressed any more?"

"No — thanks to you. Meeting you made me see everything in a different light."

"I'm glad."

"I'll never forget you, Dale," she said softly. "Will I see you again soon?"

"Yes."

"Where?"

"I'll come back to San Francisco," I

said. I hung up and then called Captain Halls.

"Thanks for getting in touch, Shand," he said. "We'll see what we can do about tracing this man Jones. Are you saying there's a connection with the inquiries you're making?"

"I'm not saying it does or doesn't connect. I merely thought you ought to be put in the picture, Captain. If there *is* a connection I'd appreciate knowing — or is that asking too much?"

"Ordinarily, yeah, but I'm willing to junk the rules in your case — just this one time, anyway. Call me back — say in a couple hours."

I took a second shave, changed into a navy mohair suit and a new white shirt with a button-down collar, and ate a steakhouse dinner. Then I made the call.

Halls said tersely: "We've made inquiries at the apartment block. Art Jones hasn't been seen there in three weeks. The manager thinks he took a powder. It happens times. He could be in Vegas. We're trying to find out from the law up there."

I was silent for a moment.

Halls said: "Sump'n on your mind?"

"Just the time factor — it's three weeks since Alvin Day went over the Golden Gate Bridge."

Halls said acutely: "You mean, Art Jones faded after pushing Day off the bridge?"

"Maybe. It's a theory worth looking into."

"We'll look," answered Halls.

8

IT was nearly ten o'clock at night when I parked on the wide apron out front of the Gilded Slipper Club and walked into a foyer big enough for a medium-sized ballroom.

The floor had a powder-blue fitted pile which flowed round fluted columns to lap the distant walls like a well-bred surf. A vivid redhead, one of three fetching girls elegantly poised behind a curved reception desk, eyed me with the patrician air of royalty condescending to notice the presence of a plebeian subject.

"Are you a member, sir?"

With the fine old Shand courtesy I resisted the impulse to announce that I would not be personally interested in taking out membership even if offered for free. Instead, I said amiably: "Unfortunately, no."

Vivid blue eyes surveyed me for a moment from behind splendid eyelashes which may have been genuine, though this seemed improbable.

"Members only are admitted, Mr . . . "

"Paraphrasing a distinguished compatriot from way back, the name isn't Doghouse Reilly."

"No . . . " She seemed uncertain how to cope.

"Not to make a mystery of it any longer, the name is Dale Shand."

"If you're visiting Los Angeles I can issue you with a temporary membership at a reduced subscription. Fifty dollars."

I passed over the money, signed the membership book and took possession of an embossed membership card with gilt edges, reflecting that fifty bucks seemed a high price to pay for what would probably be my only visit to the place. On the other hand I might acquire more than fifty dollars worth of information.

A slim young fellow with almost white hair and curiously expressionless

125

eyes took his mess-jacketed shoulders off one of the fluted columns and moved dancingly across the floor.

"Can I help you, sir?" His voice, slightly high-pitched, stopped just short of being a simper.

I said: "It depends on the nature of the help you're offering, I think."

"You want to dine, listen to the band, dance, play the tables — we got it all."

"I'll just cruise the joint while I decide what to do."

"If you're looking for a girl . . . " He let the rest of it drift.

"Why, do you provide them?"

"No, we aren't that kind of club. On the other hand, we don't bar them — if they've got class, what I mean. And nothing takes place on the premises."

"You mean one takes the lady to a hotel or goes to her apartment?"

The white-haired boy moved both hands in a gesture, smiling as he did it. "Meanwhile, your first drink is on the house. Just show your membership card to the bar waiter."

I went through double doors at the far end of the foyer into a wide room containing a cocktail bar, a band shell on which a seven-piece group was playing soft sophisticated night music, and artistically scattered tables.

I went diagonally to the bar, ordered a Manhattan and half-turned to let my eyes range over the revellers. They seemed to represent a fairly wide cross-section of free-spending citizenry — from the young guys and dolls in their expensive denims through business executives in conservatively cut suits to women in their thirties and forties whose elegantly casual exteriors had been acquired by unremitting effort and matching cost. Wasn't it Sophie Tucker who once said something to the effect that from birth to twenty-five a girl needed good looks, from twenty-five to thirty-five a good personality, from thirty-five to forty-five good clothes and from forty-five onwards good cash. I grinned at the remembered words, adding the mental footnote that this seemed a more than likely place to fulfil the final requirement.

But Mitzi Bellson wasn't among those present.

I glanced at my watch. It showed twenty minutes of eleven p.m. Maybe she was giving the place a miss tonight. Then, suddenly, she was coming through the double doors wearing a black crêpe suit with batwing sleeves and carrying a short fur. I recognized her instantly; the resemblance to the photograph was unmistakable.

She walked up to the bar, standing almost alongside me. I said equably: "We haven't been formally introduced, but may I have the privilege of buying you a drink?"

She turned slowly, her candid eyes making a rapid inventory of my appearance. Then she smiled, a long red-lipped smile against small even teeth.

"Why not?" she said. "I'll have an Alabama Fizz."

I said: "I thought I knew the composition of most drinks, but that one must have eluded me."

"The juice of half a lemon, one-and-a-half ounces dry gin and a dash of granulated sugar. Shake well with cracked ice and strain into a chilled eight-ounce highball glass. Fill with carbonated water and stir. Decorate with two sprigs of mint. Serve with straws."

"Sounds swell, Miss Bellson."

That threw her slightly. "How do you know who I am?"

"A mutual acquaintance said I was pretty sure to meet up with you here."

"Oh — what mutual acquaintance?"

"Ted Lally."

"Oh?" she said again. "And what else did he tell you?"

"He mentioned that you were an exceptionally attractive and agreeable girl."

"I see — though that still doesn't explain how you knew who I was, does it?"

"He showed me a snapshot picture of you. That's how I recognized you."

"What do you want with an attractive and agreeable girl?"

"Conversation."

The Alabama Fizz arrived. She sipped some of hers, put the glass down and said coolly: "I'm here on business."

"That makes two of us, though the nature of our respective businesses probably differs."

"I got the idea that you were trying to pick me up, whoever you are."

"The name is Dale Shand. I'm a private eye, shamus or gumshoe."

"A peeper?" She finished her drink fast. "I don't believe I have anything to say to a peeper."

"Two C notes say you have, Miss Bellson. I'm warming them for you."

"Two hundred to talk and not go to bed with me?"

"That's right."

"You're not being very flattering, are you, Mr Shand?"

"I've got eyes and they tell me that you're a very pretty girl. But right now my interest is in talking with you — not here."

"You want to come to my apartment just to talk?"

"Yeah."

"About what?"

"Something that concerns us both."

"What does that mean?"

"I'll tell you — later."

Mitzi Bellson made a small laugh. "It seems kind of an expensive conversation — but, all right, if that's what you want." She finished the rest of her drink and said: "Okay — let's go. That is, after you've played the tables. Just once will be enough."

"I get it — if you link up with a guy here you're obligated to introduce him to the gaming-room."

"If it annoys you we can call the whole thing off. On the other hand, you might hit a winning streak."

I did. Inside ten minutes I was $300 ahead of the house. In another ten minutes I was $400 down. Time to quit.

We were crossing the foyer when I noticed a man eyeing us, a well-built man with a smoothly shaved face. I couldn't recall having seen him before, but in some odd way the features were vaguely familiar.

I said: "The fellow who's looking this way, over at the reception — who is he?"

"That's Lew Packard. He works here."

"Doing what?"

"I'm not sure. I think he's some kind of floor manager. Why?"

"I just wondered. Where do I drive you?"

"I've an apartment in Glendale — Six Two Four Five Delahay Avenue. I came here by taxi."

I drove there. It was a private entrance apartment in the twenty-seven hundred block. Mitzi Bellson got lights on as we went in. The lights showed Swedish functional furniture arranged on a sea-green fitted carpet. There was a small bar in a corner by the french window. She went behind it and said: "I'm having an old-fashioned. And you?"

"Similar, Miss Bellson."

"You may as well call me Mitzi." She fixed the drinks, handed one to me and said: "Now — what do you want to talk about?"

"A man named Alvin Day. I understand you knew him."

Her hand tightened on the glass and for a moment she didn't answer. Then she said slowly: "Alvin's dead, but I guess you know that."

I nodded.

"It was in the papers. He jumped off the Golden Gate Bridge in San Francisco."

"So the police said, and the coroner's inquiry established that it was suicide."

She lit a luxury length cigarette with a book match, blew the flame out and said: "Yes, I read that."

"What's your view, Mitzi?"

133

"What makes you suppose I have any particular view?"

"You knew him — quite well — didn't you?"

"Yes, I knew Alvin."

"His widow doesn't accept that it was suicide. She asked me to investigate the circumstances. That led me to you."

"You mean she knows about me?"

"No, she doesn't know."

"Are you going to tell her?"

"It may become necessary, but I'll try to avoid it. Larraine Day says she had a good married life. I don't want to spoil her memories if I can help it."

"I think you'd better tell me exactly what has been happening, Mr Shand . . . Dale."

I told her. When I was through I added: "It could be suicide, accident — or homicide."

"Yes . . . " She spoke the word as if talking to herself.

I said: "One major question — did Alvin Day strike you as a man who would take his own life?"

134

"No!" She said it with a small vehemence, then went on: "But what I think doesn't necessarily mean anything, does it? Unlikely persons commit suicide, don't they?"

"Yeah, but the fact that you will have known a fair number of men could mean that you're in a position to form an estimate of a man's character."

"Perhaps — perhaps not. The men I meet have only one thing in common, you know — they merely want me physically, so they don't show other sides to their character."

"Just the same, you must have formed an impression of Day. How *did* he strike you?"

She mashed her unfinished cigarette in a glass tray, turning it round and round in a grey blur of ash. Finally, she looked up and said levelly: "Alvin was vigorous, articulate, decisive and opinionated, with a sense of humour which could sometimes be cutting. When I read that he had leaped off the bridge I simply couldn't believe it."

135

"You think he fell accidentally — or the other thing?"

"I've no proof, not even the start of a clue. But from what I came to know about Alvin I'd say it was murder."

"Larraine Day also thinks that, though her assessment of him is different. She says he was quiet, home-loving and a good husband."

"Maybe he had the Jekyll and Hyde syndrome. Some married men do. It's not uncommon."

"Except that husbands given to playing around aren't usually noted for being home-lovers?"

"That's true generally, I guess — but every once in a while you get one who is, the man who wants the best of both worlds. Though at some stage they usually betray themselves — and I gather that he didn't."

"Apparently not. By the way, did you like him?"

"Up to a point."

"What's that mean?"

"He was fun to be with — pleasant

without seeming to force it, affectionate without being crude. He was also generous with money and gifts. But I always felt that beyond that point there was something else."

"Like what?"

"Another kind of man, an altogether tougher man — ambitious, even ruthless if he felt he had to be." She laughed. "It's just a feeling I got . . . I could be wildly wrong."

I pondered what she had said for a moment. All that surfaced was the reflection that there had been more to Alvin Day than he let most people, including his wife, see.

Mitzi Bellson said suddenly: "You don't look the kind of man who'd be a friend of Ted Lally's."

"I didn't know him until today — Day's office manager put me on to him."

"I don't think I quite follow that."

"His name's George Lane. He chanced to see you in a parked car with Day — embracing. Incidentally, it seems like an unusual spot for you to be doing that."

She laughed again. "Well, well! I remember that time. Alvin was feeling amorous and stopped the car for a few minutes on the way back here from taking me out to lunch. And that was unusual — taking me to lunch. There was always the risk of being seen by someone who knew him — and his wife."

"Lane said you were a strikingly attractive girl and volunteered that Lally would probably know who you were. It turns out that Lally once called at Day's office and Lane knew his reputation as a playboy."

"So you called on him and Ted Lally, as it were, told all?"

"He'd met Day by chance in San Diego when they were staying in the same hotel. Day wanted to be introduced to a girl and Lally thought you might be agreeable."

"I see."

"You went with Day on a number

of occasions, I take it?"

"Five times, always here in this apartment, apart from that one time he took me out to lunch. He always left around four-thirty, except the time in San Francisco . . . "

I said sharply: "San Francisco — you haven't mentioned that."

"I'm mentioning it now," she answered coolly.

"When was this?"

She looked directly at me and said: "The night before he went over the side of the bridge."

"I think," I said quietly, "I think you'd better tell me more."

"Yes. Well, the situation was that Alvin had a two-day business trip to San Francisco. I guess you know he was only away from home overnight on rare occasions. He thought the opportunity was too good to pass up and asked me to go with him. He wanted me to stay the two nights but this would have been difficult as he had a late business dinner lined up for the second night. So it was arranged that I should stay with him just the first night.

She looked down at her spread hands. "It would've been better if I *had* stayed the second night — he wouldn't have walked on to the bridge. Incidentally, nothing I read in the papers said *why* he did that . . . "

"No — though both the cops and the coroner were satisfied that he walked on to the bridge in order to jump off it."

"I don't believe it. I don't think you do, either. He was an exceptionally strong-minded man. If he had troubles he'd fight his way out of them."

"Did he have any troubles?"

"I never knew of any."

"The business associate he was supposed to be seeing — did he say who it was?"

"No . . . " She paused, her smooth face puckering. "I remember something. There was a telephone call when we went into the hotel restaurant for

140

dinner. They paged him — you know, *will Mr Alvin Day kindly go to the telephone?* I thought it might be from his wife, but when he came back he said it was just a business call."

"Did he say who the caller was?"

"He said it was a man named Jones . . . " She broke off, staring. "Have I said something?"

"I told you about Eddie Ryker and an acquaintance of his being missing. I didn't bother to tell you his name, but it's Jones."

"There are an awful lot of people named Jones. It could be coincidence."

"It could, but I don't like coincidence when a man's life is involved."

"My goodness, are you saying that this man Jones pushed Alvin off the bridge?"

"I'm not saying it as a fact — but I'm looking at the possibility."

"I think we'll have another drink," Mitzi said.

"I'll fix them this time." I stood up, moving briskly at an angle — as a spear of orange flame erupted. The wide window was shattered and a bullet slammed into the armchair I had just left.

I threw myself headlong to the carpet, clawing for my Colt and yelling: "Stay right where you are but keep your head down."

I jumped the gun into aiming position, freeing the catch. Running footsteps sounded along the front of the apartment. I pelted for the entrance and yanked the door open as a car started, accelerating down the street. Headlights from an on-coming car glared and for a split second I saw the gunner's face as he glanced backwards. It was bearded, like the face of the man who had tried to kill me before. Then the car was gone.

I walked back into the living-room.

"It's all right, Mitzi, he's gone."

She stood up. I poured brandy for her. She sipped it, the glass rattling against her small teeth.

"It's all right," I said again. "He

wasn't shooting at you, it was me he was after." I made a twisted grin. "If you hadn't suggested another drink he'd have plugged me where I sat. I just happened to move sideways as he fired."

"But . . . but who . . . "

"A well-built number with a beard."

Mitzi stared. "You said a man with a beard tried to run you down in a car."

I screwed my eyes together trying to call up an image. When I opened them I said: "Yeah, only it occurs to me that the beard could be a fake. I'm trying to visualize what he looks like without it."

"And?"

"I think I know. Also, he has a mole on the right cheek, high up — I saw it in the lights of an approaching car."

"Well?"

"Lew Packard has a mole on the right cheek."

She uttered a small sound. Then:

"He was looking at us when we left the club."

"That's right. By the way, who owns the place?"

Her face puckered again. "That's a funny thing. Nobody ever sees him."

It was my turn to stare. "He must have a name!"

"He's simply known as Mr X. He has a private residential suite on the premises and runs the club from it. Nobody ever gets to see him, except Lew Packard and Danny Schultz."

"Who's he?"

"The white-haired boy who goes around in a white mess-jacket. I don't like him." She made the smallest shiver. "Do you think Packard had something to do with Alvin's death?"

"I'm now tasting the theory, Mitzi."

She touched my sleeve briefly. "They could be dangerous people, Dale."

"Also not as smart as they think they are. If they'd just sat tight and said and done nothing I wouldn't have connected them with Day."

"No." She looked at me. "Oughn't we to call the police?"

"If you want."

"Not particularly. I can't say I go for the idea of having cops all over my apartment."

"Besides, he missed me," I said cheerfully. "And nobody seems to have heard the shot. I guess your near neighbours must be out."

She looked at the bullet hole in the window. "I'll put sticky tape over that until I can get it fixed properly."

"Send me the invoice. If I hadn't been here it wouldn't have happened. Meanwhile, thanks for all you've told me. I now owe you two Cs."

I got my billfold out, but she shook her head. "Just for once I'm not taking money from a man . . . well, from one man, anyway."

"A deal is a deal, Mitzi."

"A deal can be cancelled and I'm cancelling it. I liked Alvin. Put the finger on the man who killed him and I'll take that as payment."

9

AT nine o'clock the next morning I called the Humbert Arms in New York. A woman with a slightly prissy voice answered.

I said without preamble: "Dale Shand calling from Los Angeles. Do you have a Mr Albert Fisher staying at the hotel?"

"We did have, sir — but Mr Fisher left several weeks ago."

"You don't happen to know where he went, or do you?"

"As a matter of fact, yes. Mr Fisher said he was going to Chicago."

"Did he leave a forwarding address for mail?"

"I suggested that to him, but he said he wasn't expecting any letters and, in any case, he wouldn't be staying long in Chicago. I'm sorry, sir."

"That's all right, it's not your fault."

"If he's a friend of yours, sir . . . "

"I could contact him at his permanent home? Unfortunately, I don't know it — I've never met him. His name was given to me in connection with a business matter."

"Oh, I see."

"How long did he stay with you?"

"Two weeks, including the night he was away on some business."

"Did he mention where?"

"He said he had to go to San Francisco but would be back the next day. Actually, it was late the following evening."

A long chance thought moved in my mind. I said evenly: "I'm starting to wonder if I've got the right Mr Fisher. Can you describe him?"

"Sure can. Around forty, rather well-built, average height . . . " She paused. Then, uncertainly: "But if you've never met him how does that help?"

"His appearance was described to me by a mutual friend. I was just checking. The Fisher I'm interested in has a mole fairly high up on the right cheek."

"Then it's the same Mr Fisher. He has a mole — I remember noticing it."

"Thanks," I said. The long chance had come off.

"You're welcome. I'm only sorry we can't furnish you with his present address."

I hung up and sat looking at the telephone without seeing it. Thoughts whirled. Uppermost was the fact that Lew Packard had posed as Albert Fisher in order to give eye-witness testimony that Alvin Day had thrown himself off the bridge — and had equipped himself with a fictitious identity and a hotel address in New York City. Why? I'll find out, I thought grimly.

Then there was Bakso, ex-Lieutenant Bakso — Why hadn't he mentioned that he was on his last day with the San Francisco police? Why had he left his office to make a telephone call from a pay booth? Perhaps he had merely thought it unnecessary to tell me he was quitting the police. Perhaps he didn't fit in anywhere. Just the same, a second talk might turn out to be useful. Well, Bakso was now living in Los Angeles, having told Captain Halls that he was taking a job with a security outfit — not saying which one. But Charles Forbes had a list of names and I called them, one after the other. Inside fifteen minutes I was in possession of the interesting information that none of them had an operator named Bakso on the payroll.

I got back to Forbes and at his suggestion called Dee Mays, a private inquiry man to whom he occasionally delegated routine work.

Mays was in. He said: "What can I do for you?"

"An ex-police lieutenant from San Francisco is now living here in L.A. Name of Bakso." I spelt it out, adding: "Can you find his address for me?"

"Should be able to. It'll take a little time, though — unless he's staying in a hotel. Other than that I'll have to contact every apartment, maybe even rooming-houses."

"I shouldn't think he's living in some crummy walk-up. Either a hotel or a decent apartment. Do your best."

"I'll call you back, say around three this afternoon," he said.

I had just put the receiver down when there was a knock on the door. I opened it on a couple of guys with the hard unblinking stare they acquire as regulation issue down at Central Homicide.

The taller of them, who wore a well-tailored grey suit, said: "Mr Shand, Mr Dale Shand?"

"Yeah, the same."

"Captain Blair with Lieutenant Ito, Los Angeles Police Department." He produced credentials. "May we come in?"

"I can't stop you, Captain."

A smile lived briefly on his heavy features. "Strictly speaking, no. But one likes to observe the decencies."

He strode into the room, a big,

well-dressed urbane man. Lieutenant Ito was three inches shorter and thin with it. He wore a crumpled sport jacket and faded blue trousers. His tight pale face wore a hostile look.

I said, echoing Ted Lally: "In what way can I brighten your lives, gentlemen?"

Blair made a dry chuckle. "Our information is that you could have lost your life last night."

"I *could*?"

Ito sneered. "Don't go coy on us, Shand. Somebody tried to gun you down. We got the tip-off."

Blair said: "The janitor at an apartment block in Glendale thought he heard a muffled shot but nobody reported anything, so he concluded he had made a mistake. But this morning he found a hole in the window of an apartment occupied by a girl named Mitzi Bellson. He figured it was made by a bullet and called us about it. We've checked with Miss Bellson, who had your hotel address. She

151

told us you decided not to call us. Why?"

"Somebody did fire a shot. It missed me. I thought perhaps it was just some kid fooling around. I didn't see anybody with a gun. I decided to let it ride."

"You had a duty to report the circumstances — you know that."

"I apologize. As I said, I figured it was just someone fooling around. Incidentally, it was a rifle shot."

"How do you know it was a rifle?"

"The slug went into an armchair. I picked it up." I felt in a pocket, came up with the bullet and handed it over.

Blair looked at it. He nodded, then said: "Someone triggers a rifle. It could be some punk kid fooling around with it, or not. But either way we should've been informed. By the way, what were you doing in the apartment?"

"Yeah, how about that?" Ito sneered again. "The girl's a hooker."

Blair said: "A high-class hooker, but

still a hooker — though, I'm guessing you were there for another purpose."

"I was there on a case. I thought it possible that Miss Bellson might be in a position to give me some information."

Blair fingered his tie. "I think you'd better explain that," he said.

I sighed. "I don't seem to have much option. I'm a private investigator visiting Los Angeles. I've been engaged by a Mrs Larraine Day to investigate the circumstances of her husband's death by falling off the Golden Gate Bridge in San Francisco."

"Alvin Day, a Los Angeles business-man," Blair said. "I recall the case. A suicide. What makes his widow want it investigating?"

"She isn't satisfied that it *was* suicide."

Ito stared. "She wouldn't go to the expense of hiring a gumshoe if it was just an accident, so she must figure it was murder."

I said nothing.

"How does Miss Bellson come into it?" asked Blair.

"She was acquainted with Day," I answered.

Ito made a strident laugh. "You'll have to do better than that, pal. You mean he was laying her."

I said nothing again.

"*Was* he, Shand?" This from Blair.

"That would appear to be the position."

"How do you come to know her?"

I explained, adding: "I was interested in getting more background on Day and thought she could supply it. She told me that he didn't strike her as the kind of man who would take his own life. That was also the view of his wife. Miss Bellson also said that while she was with him in San Francisco he got a telephone call from a man named Jones."

"The guy you say is missing?"

"Unless it's another Jones — the name is common enough. But a man named Art Jones who knew Eddie

Ryker left San Francisco, apparently for Vegas, around the time Ryker was shot dead."

"Are you saying this Art Jones killed him?"

"I'm not saying it as a fact. I'm simply considering it. I reported the circumstances to Bernard Halls, the captain of detectives in San Francisco."

"I know Halls — a good operator. What did he say?"

"He appreciated being given what information I had. He said they would try to find Art Jones in liaison with the Las Vegas law."

"I can't figure where this man Ryker gets into it. Are you working on the idea that he may be linked in some way with the inquiries you're making about Day?"

"I'm trying to find out if there *is* a link."

"Meaning that Ryker saw what actually happened on the bridge and was killed because of it?"

"You're reading me, Captain. But

there's no proof — yet."

"Miss Bellson wasn't able to give you a lot of help, I take it?"

"She formed a definite personal assessment which suggested to her mind that Alvin Day did not and could not have committed suicide."

"Well, suicide or homicide, it took place outside our jurisdiction. That would seem to let us out — but for the attempt to shoot you while you were in Miss Bellson's apartment. It *could* have been some kid fooling around with a rifle. On the other hand, it could be something else again."

"And whatever it was it happened in our neck of the woods," Ito said.

"Yeah, it did."

"And you didn't call us — shame on you, pal."

Blair said slowly: "Apart altogether from the Alvin Day case, is there anyone in L.A. who might want to have you removed from the scene — permanently?"

"I can't think of anyone. I don't even

live in Los Angeles or even in the States elsewhere, if it comes to that. I live in London. I'm over here on holiday."

"A working holiday, the ways things have taken shape."

Ito said: "If you'd called us right away we might've caught up with the guy who tried to shoot you." His thin mouth twitched. "We might even have picked him off for you."

"No way — with the new guidelines you fellows have to observe."

Ito made a spitting sound without actually spitting.

I said: "Thirty suspects shot dead by the police in a nine-month period, so the authorities put out a warning that a reverence for human life shall guide officers in considering the use of deadly force. I quote."

"We don't need you to recite the rules to us," Ito said tightly.

Blair smiled. "Critics have been saying that some officers may be trying to live up to their television and movie image as tough cops. But, in fact, a lawyer for the Los Angeles Police Association has gone on the record as welcoming the change in policy. Also, an officer can still open fire to protect himself or others or to apprehend an escaping felon who has committed a violent crime and whose escape presents a substantial risk of death or serious bodily injury to others. I also quote. Incidentally, we're not all trigger happy, but we do have to face the possibility of death — unlike those who criticize us."

I reflected that I hadn't said anything about Lew Packard. But, then, I had no proof, had I?

Blair said, suddenly: "What do you know about Big Jim Banna?"

"Only what a lawyer friend told me — that Banna runs an assortment of rackets here, the numbers racket through so-called protection to call houses. Why?"

"I just wondered whether you got in his way somehow."

"And he puts out a contract for a

hit man to fire a rifle at me?"

"It could happen, Mr Shand."

"Sure, if I'd tangled with him, which is next door to impossible since I live in England. Anyway, I've never met Banna."

"Alvin Day could have been in some trouble with the mob," Ito said.

"It doesn't seem likely. He ran a respectable business."

"Solid citizens have been known to get out of line, particularly when they start playing around."

"You mean that Banna's organization could have been blackmailing him and he wouldn't pay so they bump him off? It's possible, the way anything is possible — but I'd say it's unlikely, if only on account of Day got dead several hundred miles away in San Francisco."

"From Banna's point of view it might've been a convenient place," Blair said dryly. "But that's only speculation." He paused, then went on: "There's something else that interests us. A new syndicate is emerging in L.A., very much under cover but it's in being and Banna doesn't like it."

"I can't see Alvin Day being the victim of a syndicate," I said, less than accurately.

Ito said: "It don't signify what you can't see, pal. Day could of fallen foul of either outfit. A guy like that, cheating on his wife, could get into real trouble."

Blair turned a heavy gold ring on the third finger of his left hand. "I'm not saying that's the way it is, but it just could be like that. If you come up with anything which seems to bear it out we'll want to know."

"You have that undertaking, Captain." I thought for a second and added: "I take it that right now you don't know who is behind this new syndicate?"

"Not yet — we will, though."

"And if somebody else comes after you with a gun call us," Ito said.

"Maybe it'd be better if I fired

first and to hell with the guidelines,"
I grinned.

★ ★ ★

I ate a leisurely lunch, laying out the
facts in my mind. They still didn't make
a pattern, but I had the feeling that they
were moving in that direction . . .

The head waiter drifted up. "Telephone call for you, Mr Shand. You
can take it at the table."

"Thanks."

"You're welcome." He wheeled the
telephone up.

A voice said briskly: "Dee Mays
here — I completed inquiries a little
early."

"And?"

"Fred Nordlinger, the head man of
one of the insurance outfits, was in the
Golden Slipper Club between ten and
twelve last night and heard one of the
executives there being addressed as Mr
Bakso."

"Thanks again. I'm grateful."

Mays seemed to hesitate before asking: "Is the information important to you?"

"I don't know. It could be. Did your friend Nordlinger say what he looked like?"

"I didn't ask him — I should have done. If you want to speak to Nordlinger I'll give you his telephone number." Mays said what it was.

I called the number. A woman's voice said: "Mr Nordlinger has just come in. Hold on, I'll put you through. What name shall I say?"

"Dale Shand, a private investigator from London, in Los Angeles on a visit."

Nordlinger came on the line. "Hello, Mr Shand. What can I do for you?"

"I'm trying to locate a man named Bakso, recently of San Francisco, now living in L.A. Dee Mays says you heard someone in the Golden Slipper Club being addressed by that name."

"That's right, I did. Guy in a midnight blue tux. I figured he was something to do with the management."

I said carefully: "He may or may not be the same man. Can you describe him?"

"Sure can. Thinnish build, stiff brown hair and blue eyes, kind of hard eyes. Check?"

"Yeah, it checks."

"You want to know something else, I thought he looked like a cop or an ex-cop, despite the elegant tux."

"You're observant, Mr Nordlinger."

"Was Bakso with the police in San Francisco?"

"Yes, he resigned to take up some appointment here. I thought it was a security job, but it seems not."

"He could be handling security for the club, though places like that normally use one of the established security agencies."

"So I would have thought. Anyway, thanks."

"Happy to be of service." Nordlinger paused, then asked directly: "What's it all about — or don't you want to say?"

"No reason why not. I had a conversation with Bakso before he left San Francisco and wanted to contact him again — just a point which has arisen in connection with a case I'm engaged on. Unfortunately, I didn't know his address in L.A."

"What's the case?" asked Nordlinger equably.

I thought for a moment, then decided. "A Los Angeles businessman named Alvin Day fell, jumped or was pushed off the Golden Gate Bridge."

"Read about it. I thought the coroner's inquiry established suicide."

"It did. But Day's widow doesn't go along with the verdict."

"What does she think it was — murder?"

"She doesn't exclude that possibility."

Unexpectedly, Nordlinger said: "I met Day two-three times. That was a while back. He didn't strike me as a man who would kill himself."

"How *did* he strike you, Mr Nordlinger?"

"Quiet, self-assured, possibly with a strain of toughness which he kept out of sight. Of course, that's only an impression. I could be wrong. Also, people sometimes act out of character — so he may have committed suicide. What do *you* think?"

"I'm not sure — I'm trying to find out."

"Not easy in view of the coroner's verdict and the lapse of time."

"That's a fact, but I've a feeling that something will emerge if I try hard enough."

"The improbable takes a few days, the impossible takes a little longer, eh?"

"So they say. By the way, I take it you don't know the identity of the Mr X who runs the Gilded Slipper Club?"

"The whisper on the grapevine is that he's a big time financier who took the place over fairly recently and apparently thinks his image might suffer if it became known that he dabbles in night club ownership. Why?"

"I just wondered," I said.

I slid the receiver back on its rest and sat for a while in thought. Maybe it was time for an interim talk with Larraine Day? She might recall some small thing — meaningless if considered in isolation but just possibly having a bearing on what had been happening since I took the case.

I went out to my rented car. An all-white Cadillac was parked just in front of it. As I crossed the sidewalk the door swung open and a voice said bleakly: "Inside, Mr Shand . . ."

10

I STOOD where I was. The voice went on: "No fancy pants, Mr Shand. My friend in the back has a nine-shot Luger. It's looking at you."

"I can see it," I said shortly. I glanced both ways along the sidewalk. Unusually, it was deserted.

The man behind the steering-wheel said: "If Slim has to trigger the cannon it'll blow a hole big enough to take a Greyhound bus. You better get in."

I got in. The man with the Luger, a smoothly shaved man wearing a splendidly cut suit of middle grey, frisked me. He put my Colt on the far side of the seat and said: "No violence is contemplated — you're just taking a friendly trip."

"Yeah? Do you usually issue friendly invitations from behind a gun?"

"That was merely to make sure you

167

got in the car. On the other hand, don't ever think I wouldn't use it, if I have to."

"I don't doubt it." I looked closely at the smooth-faced man. "I've seen you some place."

"I'm often there."

"A few days ago a lawyer friend took me along to a court hearing, just as a matter of interest — you're Slim Kramar. You beat a Robbery One rap — the judge entered a *nolle prosequi*. I thought you were lucky."

"Well organized, I'd have said. I got friends who organize things. Like arranging an alibi."

"One friend in particular — Big Jim Banna."

Kramar unleashed a grin. It had all the uninhibited *élan* of a funeral parlour.

I said: "Is that where you're taking me — to meet Banna?"

The driver said without turning his head: "You're asking questions, Mr Shand. Where you're going you'll be answering them."

"Where *are* we going — to Banna's office?"

"His house. You're being invited as a very special guest."

"Banna could've called me on the telephone."

"You might have refused."

"What — refuse a royal command?"

"You might have. This way the boss makes sure."

Banna's house was a few minutes north of Sunset Boulevard off the San Diego Freeway. I put a hand in my pocket questing for my pipe.

Kramar said amicably: "Keep the hands right where I can see them — that way we don't have no trouble."

I put my hands palms down on my knees. Culver City receded behind us, then the exit for West Los Angeles. Soon we were north of Sunset and making the turn for Sepulveda. The house was within sight of the Boulevard, an ornate modern property approached via a private roadway leading up to massive wrought-iron gates. The gates were closed. Behind them was a stucco-fronted office out of which came a young guy in dark blue jeans and a pale blue shirt with a Mexican stitched collar. He had a slightly loping walk and thick yellow hair on a head which looked as if it was packed with shabby cunning. He got the gates open and leaned on the Cadillac. "You picked him up okay then, Charley?"

"What else?" The driver's tone sounded less than friendly. "Get back in your office and call the boss on the house phone."

"I've already done it — I saw you turn into the private road and made the call right away."

"Well, get back in your cubbyhole, anyway," the driver said. He let the clutch in and started driving before Yellowhead had quit leaning on the car.

"You don't like Lee, do you Charley?" This from Slim.

"I don't like his manner. One of these days I'll . . . "

Slim said distinctly: "One of these days nothing — the boss wouldn't like it. If there's ever any rough stuff he gives the order, you know that."

Charley shrugged and drove on. He turned the Cadillac sideways alongside the main entrance. It had twin coach lamps and brass-studded double doors, approached by four wide steps. We were on the top one when the doors parted, apparently by remote control.

"This way, Mr Shand," said Slim. "Walk between me and Charley."

I went with them into a vast lounge almost screaming with trendy furniture. The obligatory private bar spanned one of the corners. Big Jim Banna was behind it with a cocktail shaker. He was 6 ft 2 ins tall and still had something of the physique of the heavyweight box-fighter he had once been. He had a bland smiling face, but the eyes were curiously flat and brilliant. Gangster's eyes.

"Glad you were able to come, Mr Shand," he said.

"I didn't come, I was brought."

"I like it better that a car was placed at your disposal." Banna finished shaking the cocktail, poured generously into tall misted glasses and handed one to me. Charley and Slim had gone.

I said genially: "What are we drinking to?"

Banna fingered his royal blue tie. It had a gold stick-pin inset with a single pearl big enough for collateral on a major loan.

"On the lowest level an amicable exchange of information — on a higher plane the start of a beautiful friendship. How about that, Mr Shand?"

"Information concerning what?" I asked acutely.

Banna nursed his glass. "You don't waste time on preliminaries, do you?"

"It's already wasted by being brought here at gunpoint," I growled.

"I apologize for the display of fire-power, but it occurred to me that otherwise you might not have been willing to come. As to wasting time you may be persuaded to revise that view."

"All right — persuade me, Mr Banna."

"A man named Alvin Day recently got very dead in San Francisco, supposedly through jumping off the Golden Gate Bridge."

"The coroner's inquiry established suicide."

"Don't go simple on me, Mr Shand. You wouldn't be handling the case if you were satisfied it *was* suicide."

"Day's widow asked me to investigate the circumstances of her husband's death. She wanted to be satisfied that it was suicide."

"That means she isn't satisfied — or wasn't when she asked you to act for her. What did *you* think?"

"At the time I took the case I had an open mind."

"What's your opinion now?"

"I've no proof that would stand up

in a court of law — but I think he was thrown off the bridge."

"And just what do you base that on?"

"A combination of events," I said non-committally.

Banna smiled. "You can do better than that," he purred.

"Meaning that if I don't you'll call in your trouble boys to work me over?"

"I could do that, but I'm hoping that we can avoid that last awesome extremity."

I grinned. "You run to a line of talk somewhat at variance with your chosen occupation."

"I'm happy that you noticed it. I don't go for gangster *patois*."

"Or ring fighter's."

"Right. There's a precedent for that though — Gene Tunney used to recite Shakespeare."

"Tunney was also a champ."

"Now you're trying to wound my vanity." Banna organized a sigh. "I did well in a series of preliminary contests, but I recognized that I didn't have championship qualities and turned to other fields of enterprise."

"Like crime?"

"In the society in which we find ourselves I prefer the word *entrepreneur*."

"Or racketeer?"

"Don't try me too far, Mr Shand." Banna drank two-thirds of his drink, put the glass down on the bar top and said: "I want all available information about Alvin Day. I don't expect to get it for free. Would two thousand dollars interest you?"

"I like two grand as well as the next man, but I'm acting for a client — so, no dice."

"I admire your professional scruples even if I don't personally go along with them. Suppose we put it in another context — I'll trade my information for yours."

I considered the proposition, decided that I had nothing to lose. Aloud, I said: "What's your interest in Alvin Day?"

"I'm facing direct competition in my business," Banna said. The brilliant eyes flickered briefly.

"Competition from whom?"

Banna lit a panatella, turning the end round and round in a match flame. He shook the match until the flame died, exhaled a thin stream of blue smoke and said: "I don't know, but someone is promoting a series of enterprises which clash head-on with mine."

"What's Day got to do with it? He's dead."

"I'm interested in finding out why he got dead."

I hung an empty pipe from my teeth. "Are you saying that this anonymous rival had Day killed?"

"We can't prove it — but we think so."

"My inquiries so far indicate that Day ran an entirely legal business."

"Sure — but we know there was another side to his character. What do *you* know about that?"

I took the pipe from my teeth and said: "Day liked women. His wife didn't know it. He was discreet in the sense that he confined his extra-marital activities to the afternoons — well, mostly."

"Slim saw him in the Gilded Slipper Club . . . "

"Day went there on the recommendation of a playboy named Ted Lally, trying to pick up a girl called Mitzi Bellson. In fact, he *did* pick her up."

"We know that — but we also think he had other reasons for being there."

"Such as?"

"We think he was on the payroll of the Mister Nobody who owns the club, that he got out of line and was rubbed-out."

"Objection: Day had a profitable legitimate business — why would he hire himself out to a night club?"

"Depends in what capacity he was operating."

I said levelly: "Are you telling me that the anonymous guy who runs the club is the brain behind the new organization?"

"It figures. Some of the people who help him run the place have pretty incriminating backgrounds — guys like Danny Schultz."

"The young fellow who acts as some kind of reception manager?"

"Yeah. There are others. It all points to the club being the headquarters of the new mob."

"With a boss nobody ever gets to see?"

Banna nodded. "So far we haven't been able to identify him, but we think there's a line through the murder of Alvin Day — which is why we come to you."

I could have asked Banna how he even knew I existed, but I didn't. Instead, I merely said: "I see."

Banna finished his drink. "Your turn now, Mr Shand."

I said: "After Day went over the side of the bridge a jazz musician named Eddie Ryker, who may have seen what actually happened, was shot dead. I found the body. At the same time a man known as Art Jones unaccountably went missing. He may have gone to Las Vegas. The San Francisco police are trying to find him with the co-operation of the law in Vegas."

Banna stared. "I don't get it — we've no information about anyone named Art Jones being linked with the organization."

"Nevertheless, Ryker was shot dead in a small musical instrument store he owned in San Francisco — and Jones, who Ryker knew, can't be found. And there's something else. Mitzi Bellson went up to San Francisco with Day. She says he was called to the telephone and that when he came back he told her the call was from a man named Jones."

"Are you going to tell me that Art Jones pushed Day off the bridge?"

"That's what I'm trying to find out."

"But you think he did?"

"I think he could have."

Banna fingered his jaw. "I'm obliged for the information. You've opened up a new line of thought. What I don't get is that we know nothing, but nothing, about any guy called Art Jones.

"And you think you would know if he was part of this new mob?"

"Yeah . . . unless he's a hit man from San Francisco and they gave him a contract." Banna's eyes flickered. "That could be it. Hell, it must be. That would explain why we don't have a line on him."

"It's possible."

"I'd say it's virtually for sure — and I appreciate your telling me." Banna took out his billfold. It was fat with hundred dollar bills. He started peeling some off.

I shook my head. "You don't owe me anything, let's just say we traded information. Yours was as interesting to me as mine was to you. If Alvin Day was linked with this new group it opens up a new avenue of thought for me."

Banna said slowly: "We got contacts in San Francisco and Vegas — I'll get some inquiries moving."

"If Art Jones *did* push Day off the bridge how is that going to help you find the brains behind the rival organization?"

Banna smiled bleakly. "I'm guessing that Jones knows the identity of this Mr X. If he does maybe we can persuade him to talk it up for us."

"Suppose I find out first?"

"I make you an offer for your knowledge, and I don't mean peanuts."

I grinned. "You might not know that I know."

Banna's mouth twitched momentarily. "We'll know," he said cosily.

11

LARRAINE DAY was backing her car when I drove up. She keyed the ignition off, got out and said: "I was just going to the supermarket, but it can wait. We'll go into the house."

She led the way in, turned and said: "Well?"

I put it in a sentence. "I have reason to believe that your husband didn't take his own life, Mrs Day."

She sat on the settee with her hands folded in her lap. "Tell me exactly what you've found out, Mr Shand."

"A man named Albert Fisher told the San Francisco police that he saw your husband jump off the bridge. Fisher made a statement and subsequently left for New York. When I telephoned the hotel he had been staying at there he had left, apparently for Chicago. I then went on the bridge myself, just to see the actual spot. Something happened."

"What?"

"I saved a girl from throwing herself off the bridge, a girl named Judy Gresham. It turned out that she had been on the bridge before — at the time your husband was also there." I told her the rest, the way it had happened — everything except the fact that Alvin Day had been with Mitzi Bellson.

Larraine Day listened in silence. Even when I had finished she didn't reply immediately. She seemed to be turning everything round and round in her mind. But finally she said: "This Miss Gresham saw my husband approaching the side of the bridge, then the fog blotted out her view. But she thinks there was an eye-witness apart from this man Fisher — the man you say was called Eddie Ryker, the man you found murdered."

"Yes."

She looked hard at me. "Are you

telling me that Eddie Ryker saw what really happened and was killed because of it?"

"It's a tenable theory, Mrs Day."

"Now you're being cautious. It *must* be so."

"Eddie Ryker could've been shot for some other reason. I agree it's not probable, but I don't want to put theories up as hard facts."

"Just the same, you think Alvin was murdered?"

"I think that, yeah."

"Then what are you going to do?"

"Find out. Incidentally, or maybe not incidentally, another man comes into the picture."

"You haven't so far mentioned that . . . "

"I was coming to it. I don't know precisely how this other man fits in. All I've been able to discover is that he knew Ryker — and has literally vanished, though he may be in Las Vegas. The police are looking for him there."

"Do you or they think he killed my husband?"

"We don't know, but he fits in somewhere. He's a man named Art Jones and I found out that your husband took a telephone call at his hotel in San Francisco from someone named Jones and . . . " I stopped, then said: "Do you know this man?"

"No." She shook her head.

"You looked just now as if the name meant something to you, Mrs Day."

She stood up. "I remembered something, something I'd forgotten. It comes back . . . wait a moment." She went out of the room and returned with a torn-off slip of notepaper.

I took it from her and read: *A. Jones, Apartment C, 7658 Carling Street, South San Francisco*. Immediately below the address had been written the letter R, followed by an exclamation mark.

"It's the last known address of Art Jones," I said. "Where did you find it?"

"I was going through Alvin's desk in the hope that I might find something — anything that might help. This note was wedged in an envelope which also contained an insurance premium receipt. The note must have been left there inadvertently. Alvin must have forgotten about it."

I said again: "It's the last known address of the missing Art Jones. It establishes that he is the Jones your husband took a call from in San Francisco."

"He may also be the man who killed my husband."

"It's possible. The San Francisco police are trying to follow that up. I'll have to tell them about this note."

"I thought they were satisfied that it was suicide."

"Lieutenant Bakso was."

"The officer who resigned from the force but didn't mention it when you met him?"

"That's right."

"Do you think *he's* involved in this?"

"Yes, in some way I haven't yet figured."

"The letter R — what does that mean?"

"I wish I knew. It could stand for almost anything." I fell silent for a few moments, then said: "By the way, did your husband have any business interests apart from real estate?"

"I'm certain he didn't, he'd have told me . . . why do you ask?"

"No reason, I'm just trying anything."

"I'm certain he hadn't. Alvin was never secretive — the reverse."

"Art Jones could've been a business contact," I said tentatively.

"I suppose so." She sounded vaguely troubled. "Alvin didn't mention that he was seeing anyone of that name. But he was in something of a hurry the day he left for San Francisco — he had to fit in a dental appointment, an adjustment to the partial lower denture he wore.

There was a pause. Then Larraine Day said: "Do you think you'll find this man Jones?"

"We've *got* to find him," I answered.

I drove back to the hotel, peeled off my jacket, loosened my tie and sat in a hide leather armchair arranging and re-arranging the facts like a poker player re-shuffling a deck of cards. Time passed. I had yet to deal myself a winning hand — but far down in my mind there carne the start of an idea. I picked up a scratch-pad, wrote the letter R, then the words rendezvous, recognition, reappraisal, relinquish, reproduction, rare and right. I looked at what I had written, finally ringed the last word. It was a possibility . . . but right for what?

I got out of the chair, picked up the telephone and called Ted Lally.

"Hello, Shand," he said. "Now what?"

"Just a point. You mentioned recommending Day to the Gilded Slipper Club."

"Yeah, I did." There was a sudden abrasive edge to his voice.

I didn't miss it. "Has something

occurred to irritate you?"

"You can say that again. Letting me recommend him to a place he had been to before . . ."

I said sharply: "How do you know that?"

"I had a lunchtime drink — well, several drinks — with Dave Loring, a guy I know. He had just got back from a business trip to Europe lasting several weeks. One thing led to another and I was telling him about Day and he stared and said I must be joking. I said no joke and what the hell did he mean. Then he told me that he and Day had been to the place before, more than once. I felt several kinds of a sap, I can tell you — recommending Day to a place he already knew."

"Mitzi Bellson didn't say anything about knowing Day before you introduced him."

"His previous visits must have been before that — she doesn't go to the club every night."

"Thanks," I said mechanically.

"You're welcome. But why should Day have let me make a fool of myself like that?"

"Perhaps he didn't want to admit having been there previously. Your friend is sure about Day having been to the club before? He couldn't have been mistaken?"

"No way. He knew Day on account of having done some business with him. I . . . " Lally paused. His tone changed as he said slowly: "Is the information important?"

"It's interesting."

"Was that what you were calling me about?"

"I didn't know Day had been to the club before."

"You didn't know, but you wanted to find out if he had been — check?"

"I wondered."

"If I'd known I'd have told you when you were here. So you thought I was holding out on you?"

"You have my unqualified assurance that it wasn't like that. There was just the possibility that you might have found out subsequently that he had been there — you could call it a long chance."

Ted Lally laughed, his good humour restored. "You're being too bloody careful for words. I'd say you must have heard something — or made an inspired guess."

"Maybe the latter, though I don't seem to be getting a lot of inspiration on this case."

"You've just scored with one inspiration. I'd say you have other little, thoughts at the back of that fertile mind of yours."

"I love this flattery," I said.

"I take it you're not going to tell me more?"

"That's right," I said cheerfully. "Or at least not yet."

"What's that intended to mean?"

"When I'm through I might join you in a lunchtime drink." Lally chuckled. "I'll count the moments," he said.

12

IT was 9.40 p.m. when I walked back into the Gilded Slipper Club. The white-haired boy minced towards me. He was wearing a new white mess jacket with golden epaulets. He was also wearing a new smile, phony as all hell.

He said: "Good evening, Mr Shand — a pleasure to see you again. Are you dining?"

"I've already dined."

"Gambling?"

"I doubt it."

"Dancing?"

"I doubt that, too."

"You want a girl there are several around."

"So I see."

"Mitzi Bellson hasn't shown, though." The white-haired boy leered. His eyes were like nameless sins.

192

"As a matter of fact, I'd like to talk with Lew Packard."

The boy's eyes flickered. His mouth opened to speak when Bakso came into the foyer. A new Bakso resplendent in a midnight blue tuxedo over a frilled white shirt with a deep crimson bowtie.

Seeing me stopped him in his tracks, but only momentarily. He came forward with his right hand held out. "Shand — a pleasant surprise. I didn't know you were a member."

"I achieved that high distinction last night," I said.

"You did? I wasn't told." Bakso smiled. "No reason why I should be, though — they wouldn't know we were acquainted."

"Captain Halls, with whom I had a talk in San Francisco, told me you had joined a security outfit in L.A."

Bakso waved a hand. "This is it. Well, it's not a security outfit, but I'm in charge of security for the club. You weren't looking for me, I take it. No, you couldn't be, you didn't know I was here."

"Actually, I've come to see Lew Packard," I said.

"You know him?" Bakso's voice was studiedly casual.

"Not exactly."

"I don't quite follow . . . "

"I thought it possible that Packard might be able to give some information about Alvin Day."

"The guy who jumped off the bridge — you're still working on the case, then?"

"That's right. I understand that Day was a member here."

"Oh? I didn't know that. But, then, I wouldn't — it'd be before my time. What did you want to know?"

"I'm uncertain — let's say anything Packard knows about Day. It could be something or nothing. I just want to have a talk with him."

Bakso made a small movement with his shoulders. "I guess you've left it too late. Packard is no longer working

194

here — he left today for Detroit."

"Too bad." I sighed. "What's he going to do in Detroit — manage another club?"

"All he said was that he had a deal lined up . . . he has friends there."

I said carelessly: "Well, it's not so important that I need to go to Detroit looking for him."

"I'd like to help you if I could — but, as I say, Day's visits to the club must've been before my time." Bakso signalled to the boy in the mess jacket. "Danny — you must have met a member called Alvin Day."

"Sure, Mr Bakso."

"Ask Danny anything you like, Shand."

"Just one question — did he form any friendships with other members whose names you can tell me?"

"You mean did he meet other men here socially or in any other way?"

"Yeah, did he?"

"Not that I noticed." Danny grinned meaningly. "I guess he was too busy dating Mitzi Bellson. Like you were last night, Mr Shand."

Bakso's face wore a schooled look. "I didn't know that," he said. I understood intuitively that he was lying.

"Mr Shand left the club with her," Danny Schultz said.

"But not for the purpose you think, my friend."

He shrugged, not speaking.

"I fell into conversation with Miss Bellson. It emerged that she knew Day and was willing to talk to me about him. I thought she might be able to tell me something that would help the inquiries I'm making. In the event all she could tell me was that she liked Day and had been with him on a number of occasions. I guess it wasn't any help."

An expression came and went on Bakso's face, very fast — but not so fast that I failed to identify relief.

Bakso said: "Having drawn a blank you came back here in the hope that Lew Packard could help?"

"It occurred to me that as the club manager he might know something about Day's visits here." I sighed again. "And now he's gone. Not my lucky night, I guess."

"I guess it isn't." Bakso fingered his silk-faced lapels. "It *was* suicide, you know — Day leaped off the bridge all right. Or have you found something out?"

"I've still no proof that it wasn't suicide."

"What does Halls think?"

"Same as you, Mr Bakso." It was less than the truth.

Bakso glanced at his wrist watch. "I should be circulating among the guests — part of the job. Make yourself free of the place if you're staying on. See you later perhaps, eh?"

I drifted round the club, seeing the couples on the dance floor, the diners in the restaurant and the compulsive gamblers in the gaming-room, though what I was actually looking for was a chance to go unobserved down the corridor leading to the executive suite. On my third time round I got it.

The corridor was temporarily empty with nobody anywhere near the entrance. I went down it soundlessly. There was a door at the far end. I tested it carefully, but it was on the lock. I put the palm of a hand against the panels, turning the knob. The door began to move inwards. I couldn't risk opening it more than a fraction of an inch, enough to hear but not enough to see.

A voice said: " . . . I won't need to see you again, it's complete now."

A small pause, then a different voice. "You've done a swell job, Doc. I'm grateful. This will prove it . . . "

"You're being generous . . . " Another pause. "It's a thousand more than we agreed."

"And worth every cent, my friend. A major achievement." The speaker chuckled. "A pity you can't advertise it, eh?"

"What you're paying buys total silence."

"Yes." The voice suddenly hardened. "That's the one thing you have to remember — at all times."

"You don't have to worry about that. I don't talk about what I do."

"No, it could be dangerous — for you, I mean.

There was a small sound, like a chair being moved. I went back along the corridor. Bakso wasn't near the entrance, nobody was near the entrance. I strolled into the foyer.

The girl I had spoken to on my previous visit looked up from the reception desk and said brightly: "Good evening, sir — enjoying yourself?"

"You could say that."

From where I stood I could just see the corridor. A man came down it, a cadaverous man in a navy suit. He was carrying a small black case. He had a slight stoop, could be anywhere between fifty and sixty. He crossed the foyer, nodding to the girl receptionist, and went out. After a moment a car motor started.

I said affably: "There goes one guest leaving early."

"The one who just went out?"

"That's right. For a second I thought I knew him. I guess I must have been thinking of some other fellow."

"Mr Hemsley's been here a number of times, but I don't think he's a member. Not in the usual sense, what I mean."

I smiled. "I *must* have been mistaken, I don't know any Mr Hemsley."

"You probably wouldn't, he lives in San Diego."

I shrugged indifferently. "A chance resemblance misled me." I made a small yawn. "I think I'll have a drink and then call it a day."

I went into the cocktail lounge and sat at a side table. A bar waiter hovered, mutely inquiring.

"A Manhattan," I said.

I sat nursing the drink while thoughts began to tumble through my mind, at last starting to make a pattern. When the last piece fell into place

I drove to my hotel and made two telephone calls.

The first was to Captain Blair at Police Headquarters.

I said: "Do you know anything about a doctor in San Diego named Hemsley?"

There was a pause, then Blair said carefully: "We know of him. Why?"

"I've an idea that he may be able to throw some light on Alvin Day's background."

"You mean he was a friend of Day's?"

"I'm not certain. It's possible. If he *was* a friend of Day's I may need to see him. On the other hand, maybe not. It depends."

"Depends on what?"

"On what you're about to tell me."

Blair chuckled. "I haven't said I'm about to tell you anything. What makes you think we may have him on the police blotter?"

"It was just a possibility. Have you?"

"We have some notes about him.

Nothing we could put up to the D.A. If *you* have anything I'd be interested."

"Nothing beyond the fact that he visits the Gilded Slipper Club and so may have known Day. Meanwhile, the fact that you're interested in Doc Hemsley would seem to be suggestive."

Blair said: "Hemsley isn't a medical doctor, he's a surgeon. We think he does work on the side for some of the mobs."

"Like if a hood is wounded in a police shoot-out or any other kind of shoot-out Hemsley extracts the slug and treats the injury — strictly *sub judice*?"

"So we think. What we lack is proof. If you have any we'll want to know."

"I'll remember — and that's a promise, Captain. By the way, you're working late, aren't you? I thought the day captain went home long before now."

"Something arose almost as I was reaching for my hat — a body washed ashore just north of Palos Verdes. Not a drowning. Somebody triggered a gun in the back of his head. A guy named Lew Packard, the floor manager at the Gilded Slipper Club. You don't happen to know him, by any chance?" Blair paused, waiting.

"Mitzi Bellson pointed him out to me when I was talking with her at the club, that's all. I didn't speak to him. Incidentally, I heard tonight that he had left the place to go to Detroit, to live there I mean."

"Well, if he did he never got there and now he never will. A clear case of homicide — people don't shoot themselves in the back of the head. You wouldn't have any ideas about this?"

"None," I said. It wasn't strictly true. "If I do hear anything I'll come back to you — that's also a promise."

I hung up, then called Big Jim Banna.

His voice said: "Banna here — who's speaking?"

"Shand."

"I'm in bed. I was just dropping off. What gives?" Banna's voice was heavy with sleep or with something that made it heavy.

"The cops have fished Lew Packard's body out of the ocean near Palos Verdes. There's a big hole in the back of his head."

"*What!*" The heaviness went from the voice.

"Somebody fed him a slug. It's a homicide."

"How do you come to know?"

"Blair, the captain of detectives, just told me."

"Why are you telling me?"

"I thought you might be interested."

"Why again?"

"I think Lew Packard was working for you, that's why."

"Packard worked as floor manager at the Gilded Slipper Club."

"Yeah — but you planted him there, didn't you?"

"Did you tell that to Blair?"

"No."

Banna breathed relief. Then: "What makes you think Lew was working under cover for us?"

"You knew I was acting for Alvin Day's widow. The only way you could know that was if somebody told you. Somebody like Lew Packard."

"It could of been somebody else."

"It had to be somebody at the Gilded Slipper Club. I'm guessing it was Packard. I'm damned sure it wasn't Danny Schultz."

"That punk . . . "

"Schultz couldn't know I was working for Mrs Day, but somebody did know and told you. In fact, you gave yourself away."

"Maybe — but I never mentioned Lew Packard to you."

"It was him, though, wasn't it?"

"You're guessing, Shand — you don't *know*." There was a small silence. Then Banna said: "Okay, Lew *was* working under wraps for my organization. But *we* didn't have him rubbed out."

"I never thought that. Why did you plant Packard on the club?"

"We think it's being used as a front by the rival organization. Lew's briefing was to report to us any significant circumstances."

"And I was one of the significant circumstances."

"Yeah."

"The place is run by a man nobody gets to see — apart from his chief executive, an ex-cop from San Francisco named Bakso."

"And you figured that Day was involved in some way?"

"It was a possibility."

Banna said evenly: "When Day went over the bridge we accepted that it was suicide — until Lew reported that you were taking an interest in the thing. That appeared to indicate murder . . . " Banna paused. "Day could have accidentally stumbled on something at the club."

"Like what?"

"Like the identity of the guy nobody ever sees, this Mr X."

"And Mr X puts out a contract for Day's removal?"

"It could be like that. What's your view?"

"Cloudy," I said. "There's something else. A man twice tried to kill me, once by driving a car at me and next with a high velocity rifle. He missed both times."

"You *saw* him?"

"He was wearing a beard, but he had a mole on the right side of his face, high up. When Packard was pointed out to me in the club he was clean-shaven — but he had a mole on the same side of his face. I then visualized what he would look like with a false beard."

Banna said: "He didn't have a hit contract from me — you got to believe that."

"He almost certainly got it from the mastermind of the rival syndicate."

"I don't get it. You weren't

investigating the club."

"No, I was and am investigating the presumed suicide of Alvin Day — but the inquiry led me to the club. Could be Mr X thought I might uncover something, so he issues a contract to Lew Packard."

"Lew called me on the telephone at prearranged intervals — but he didn't say anything about a contract."

"Just the same, he had one — and bungled it both times."

Banna said: "We didn't kill him, Shand."

"I never thought otherwise. You had no reason. But the Mr X mob had one — the fact that Packard reported the failure of a mission not once but twice. That made him a two-time loser and an expendable liability."

"So they rub him out."

"Yes — and that was a mistake, too, because it's brought the law in."

"They probably reckoned that the body would be washed out to sea and never found."

"They probably did — but a really smart operator wouldn't rule out the possibility."

Banna said: "You think round corners and you think ahead. There's room for a guy like you in our set-up."

"There aren't any guys like me. By the way, if Packard was accepting a contract from Mr X he was acting as a sort of double agent. You'd better watch that point next time you plant someone on your rivals."

"I'll do that. You sure you won't team up with us?"

"I'm sure, Jim."

I put the phone down and sat thinking. More jigsaw pieces were falling into place. But there were still several other things to be done. I called the Blue Note in San Francisco and asked for Al Burke.

A feminine voice said: "He's on the stand right now, but the band is due for a break in a couple of minutes. Can you hold?"

"Sure. When he comes off the stand

tell him the call is from Dale Shand in Los Angeles and that it's important, will you?"

"My pleasure, Mr Shand."

Al Burke came on the line two minutes later. I went straight to the only point that mattered. "You knew Eddie Ryker's sidekick Art Jones, didn't you?"

"Well, he wasn't exactly a buddy . . . "

"But you know what he looks like."

"Yeah, I met him a time or two. Why, is it important?"

"Only you can answer that, Al. It can't be done over the telephone. I'll need to see you in person. Look — will you meet me tomorrow for lunch at the Belvedere Hotel. Say at one o'clock. Can you be there?"

"One p.m. is about my usual time for getting up, but I'm willing to make an exception."

"I'll be there waiting, Al."

★ ★ ★

210

It was late, but I picked up the telephone and called Hemsley's home address in San Diego. I had only one question to ask. When I got the answer one of the last two pieces of the jigsaw fell into place.

13

I CAUGHT a morning flight to San Francisco, arriving with time in hand. I ordered coffee and took it at a side table in the lobby, idly turning the pages of a newspaper.

At two minutes of one p.m. Al Burke came in. I signalled him and ordered more coffee.

Burke took a facing seat and said curiously: "What's it all about, Mr Shand?"

"Art Jones. I told you that over the telephone."

"You did, but you didn't go into details." Burke stirred his coffee, adding: "I don't know much about him. I can't fill you in on his background, what I mean."

"It's not background information I want, it's something else."

"You asked if I knew what he

looked like — why?"

I took out the snapshot picture Larraine Day had given me and laid it flat on the table.

"Take a long hard look at it, Al — then tell me if you've ever seen this man before."

Burke peered closely, taking his time. Then he said: "This guy, he's almost a ringer for Art Jones."

"But not quite."

"No, not a complete ringer. The face is slightly longer — but otherwise the resemblance is close enough to be a double."

I breathed hard down my nose. "You're positive?"

"I'm positive. The likeness would fool most people."

"Especially if he was dead and had been in the ocean some little while?"

Al Burke's eyes jumped. "For Chrissake!"

"The picture is of a man named Alvin Day who is supposed to have leaped to his death off the Golden

213

Gate Bridge. A body taken from the sea was identified as his, also clothes and small personal possessions."

Burke stared. "Are you saying that it wasn't Day who was taken from the Pacific — that, in fact, it was Art Jones?"

"That's what I'm saying, Al."

"Jesus!" Burke put his cup down with a small clatter. He said: "There was a piece in the newspaper about a man named Alvin Day jumping off the bridge."

I nodded. "The coroner and the police were satisfied that it was a suicide case. Mrs Day didn't accept that her husband had taken his own life and asked me to investigate."

"What did she think it was — murder?"

"Yes."

"It couldn't be accident. People don't jump off bridges by accident. So it's either suicide or homicide."

"It also makes it something else," Al Burke said quietly. "If I'm reading you it means that Day faked his own presumed death by pushing his double off the bridge."

"You're reading me correctly, Al."

"It all figures . . . but you still don't have any proof."

"I'll get it," I said.

We were lunching in the restaurant when Al Burke grinned and said: "It's like something in a movie — except that this is for real. I take it that you don't want me to talk about this?"

"I'd prefer that you didn't — at this stage anyway."

"I'd like to know the outcome, though."

"I'll come back to San Francisco when it's all over and tell you. I'll drop by at the Blue Note for an earful of that good Dixieland jazz you play."

★ ★ ★

It was mid-afternoon when I walked in on Captain Halls at Police Headquarters.

"I've news for you, Captain," I said.

"That's more than I have for you — we haven't been able to find Art Jones."

"You haven't been looking in the right place."

Halls stared. "I thought you held the view that he went to Vegas."

"He was presumed to have gone there, but he didn't — in fact, he couldn't."

"I don't get it. If he isn't in Vegas where the hell is he?"

"In Pasadena — very dead. Specifically, his ashes are there, in the name of Alvin Day."

Halls splayed both hands on his desk. "I think," he said softly, "I think you'd better lay it on the line. In detail."

I told him everything. At the end of it he said: "If the remains have been cremated the evidence vanishes with them."

"Not quite. It hinges on one factor."

"Which is?"

"Whether the police doctor made an exhaustive examination of the body

216

believed to be Day's."

"I can answer that — he did. As a matter of fact, he's in the building right now. I'll get him to come in." Halls spoke briskly into an intercom: "Doc Brodie? Halls speaking. Can you spare a few minutes? Good. I've someone here I want you to meet — or, more accurately, he wants to meet you. It's kind of vital."

Halls sat back, lighting a cigarette. The door opened and Dr Brodie came in, a burly man in his fifties with a mane of iron grey hair and inquiring blue eyes.

"Doc, this is Dale Shand, a private investigator from London in California on a visit. He's interested in the Alvin Day case and wants to ask you something. You have complete authority to answer it."

Brodie looked at me. "Right — shoot," he said.

"Only one question, Doctor — was the man identified as Alvin Day wearing a partial lower denture?"

217

"I can answer that unequivocally. He had all his own teeth, in excellent condition for a man in early middle age."

"For God's sake," breathed Halls.

Brodie looked at me, then at Halls. "I appear to have unwittingly made a significant announcement," he said. "One of you had better explain."

"Alvin Day had a partial lower set, Doctor," I said.

Brodie looked bewildered. "There must be some mistake. I made a detailed examination. He had all his own teeth except for two at the rear which had been extracted and not replaced."

"I'm not doubting it, Doctor."

"Then what . . . " Brodie paused, his eyes widening.

"Day had a partial denture — therefore the body you examined wasn't Day's."

"But he was identified by an employee of Day's."

"What was left of it by the sharks."

"But the clothes and small personal belongings — they were Day's."

"Yeah . . . "

"If it wasn't Alvin Day who was it?"

I said slowly: "All the indications are that the remains were those of a man named Art Jones who has been missing ever since Day was presumed to have jumped off the Golden Gate Bridge. I've established that Jones was a near double." I took out the snapshot photograph.

Brodie looked at it for a long moment. Then he said: "Yes, the resemblance is quite striking. I take it that this is a picture of Alvin Day."

I nodded. "The likeness isn't total, but it's enough."

"Yes, especially when you consider the state the body was in." Brodie passed the photograph back and said: "Like you, I've just one question to put — *where is Alvin Day?*"

"Unless all my deductions are wrong

Alvin Day is alive and well and living in Los Angeles."

"You mean he induced or forced this man Jones to wear his clothes and then threw him off the bridge?"

"That's right."

"Why?"

"I think Day is masterminding a new crime syndicate in Los Angeles and needed a completely new identity."

"I'm not quite with you, Shand. He could give himself another name, but he would be recognized on the street sooner or later."

"Not if he had plastic surgery to his face."

Brodie made a breathy whistling sound.

I filled my pipe, lit it and said: "A man nobody sees, a man known to his staff simply as Mr X, is running a night club in L.A. I believe it's a front for a new criminal venture. Day is moderately well known in connection with the legitimate business he owned, so he had to assume a new appearance. Of course, he could simply have disappeared but then the hunt would be up for him. Besides, he needed to remain in Los Angeles. Better if a coroner's inquiry established that he took his own life. Then nobody is looking for him. I don't know how he came to meet up with Art Jones — probably sheer chance. But it gave him the idea. Also, it worked. Jones's mutilated body was taken from the ocean and identified as that of Alvin Day. I saw a man named Hemsley in the club last night. Hemsley is a crooked surgeon. I called him and asked if he did cosmetic surgery. He was guarded — but he said yes."

Halls said: "It all fits, but you still haven't proof that this Mr X is Day."

"Not yet."

"The police in Los Angeles will have to be told."

"I'll be seeing Captain Blair as soon as I get back. Not that the law can do anything — Alvin Day is officially dead and Mr X has merely to deny all knowledge of anyone named Alvin Day."

Halls eyed me for a moment. "Then what are you going to do?" he asked.

"I'll have to think of something," I said.

14

AT ten o'clock the next morning I telephoned the Gilded Slipper Club. A suave baritone voice said: "Yes, who's calling?"

"The name is Shand — Dale Shand."

"What can I do for you, Mr Shand?"

"I'd like to speak to Mr Bakso."

"He won't be in the club until noon."

"Perhaps I could see him then?"

"I'm afraid not. We have an important business conference scheduled for that time."

I manufactured a sigh. "Too bad. When *can* I see him?"

"Any time this evening after we open. If you care to leave a message I'll see that he gets it. Perhaps you will care to state the nature of your business?"

"It's about the late Alvin Day . . . "

A sound came down the line, a sound like an involuntary catching of breath. Then he made a mistake. "I don't believe I know anyone of that name, Mr Shand."

"He's a fellow who leaped off the Golden Gate Bridge in San Francisco a few weeks ago."

"Indeed?" The smooth voice was carefully uninterested.

"Bakso, who was in the San Francisco police at the time, handled the case. In fact, it was his last before he quit the police. He was satisfied that it was suicide."

"But you want to see him about it?"

"Yes."

"Why, is there some new development?"

"Something has come up, something which may interest him."

"I'll tell him that you will be coming in tonight."

"Thanks. By the way, to whom am I speaking?"

"To the owner of the club. I live

on the premises — I have a residential suite. Actually, I'm the only person in the club right now. But, as I say, Bakso will be coming in at noon. I'll give him your message."

"Thanks again."

At 11.30 a.m. I parked a block away from the club and walked back. The double doors at the main entrance were closed. They looked as if you would need a blast of TNT to get them open. I went down a gravelled pathway and found a smaller rear door. I got it open and slid round it. I was in what appeared to be Alvin Day's private office, judging by the expensive furniture. There was a sliding panel let into one of the walls, like a dumb waiter. I finger-tipped the panel so that it moved sideways — no more than an inch. That was sufficient. I was looking into a handsomely appointed living-room. A small sound, like someone moving, reached me. I closed the panel. I could open it again later, when Bakso came.

That was no more than minutes later. Footsteps sounded in the corridor beyond the room. Then a bell rang three times — one long, two short, like a prearranged signal. The door to the corridor opened by remote control and the suave baritone voice said: "Well, it's finalized — how do I look?"

"Like a new man — and I guess that's all you want to know, Alvin." It was Bakso speaking. He went on: "You've only just got the bandages off?"

"A couple of hours ago. The surgical wounds have healed completely, the way Hemsley said they would."

"The change in your appearance is remarkable — even your wife would be hard put to identify you."

"That's a risk I'm not proposing to take," said Day dryly.

"I was joking. Just the same, it's better you don't submit yourself to that test. Even if she didn't recognize your face she'd know your voice."

"I'm trying to change that, but it's

not the easiest thing. However, I don't anticipate meeting any of my former business associates. What'll you have to drink?"

"The usual."

"A brace of stiff whiskies coming up."

I inched the panel open again and took a darting look. Day was going behind a private bar. Bakso had his back turned to me.

I recalled what Alvin Day looked like in the snap-shot picture. The transformation was almost staggering — the changed contours of the nose, the slight but significantly new line of the mouth. There were other subtle changes, expertly wrought. In addition, the dark hair was now thickly grey — and, probably for the first time in his life, he had a moustache.

Alvin Day said: "I take it everything is set for the launching?"

"Yeah. The three properties you quietly acquired while you were in the realty business have been converted — a swell job. Staffing has been completed and we open up on Monday night as you planned."

Day's new mouth twitched fractionally. "Right in the middle of Banna's territory."

"He's not going to like it, Alvin. Sooner rather than later we're going to have trouble."

"We'll be ready for it. We've a bunch of trouble boys more than capable of dealing with the Banna mob. By the way, you'd better get out of the habit of calling me Alvin — from now on I'm Herbert Bradfield Calerson. Brad to all friends."

Day sipped some of his drink and went on: "We'll clean up big — an organized call girl circuit, bookmakers' offices, protection insurance — with menaces if necessary. We'll make several fortunes and nothing Banna is going to do will stop us."

Bakso set fire to a cigarette, blew out the match flame and said meditatively:

"Lucky we met when you visited San Francisco last fall — lucky for both of us."

Day smiled. The cosmetic surgery made him do it with the left side of his mouth only — another transformation. "Yes, a chance meeting in a night spot. As I recall it, the first of several which paved the way for our partnership in crime. I was then at the preliminary planning stage and looking for a tough operator with knowledge of the underworld."

"And met me . . . "

"A fortunate meeting. We make a perfect team. I do the overall planning, you handle the details. Incidentally, you've already earned a bonus for locating Doc Hemsley. It enabled me to assume an entirely new appearance."

"You warned Hemsley to stay clammed-up?"

"Of course. I take it there's no danger of him talking?"

Bakso laughed shortly. "I guess he knows what would happen to him if he did. He'd go the way Lew Packard did."

"We slipped up over engaging Packard, both of us," Day said.

"Everybody makes one goof. There won't be any others. Packard came with a reputation as a hit man. Some hit man — he twice failed to get Shand."

"Yes, that made him expendable." Day paused, then said: "By the way, Shand was on the telephone earlier this morning. He wants to see you."

"You spoke to him yourself?"

"There wasn't anyone else in the club. Anyway, he'd never heard my voice before."

"What exactly did you tell him?"

"I merely said I was the owner of the club and that he could see you if he cared to come along tonight."

"I'll see him."

Day said distinctly: "I don't like it that Shand is still on the case. Suppose he latches on to something?"

Bakso said calmly: "He already has."

Day's head jerked. "*What* . . . "

"Before coming here I called Hank Lee, a detective sergeant in San Francisco — an old buddy. Just a friendly chat about old times, that kind of thing. But I was really fishing for information and he let it out that Shand found Eddie Ryker shot dead in his shop after I gave it to him."

"I'm starting to wonder whether *that* was a good idea . . . "

"We had no choice. One of the bridge guards who knew Ryker slightly saw him walking off the bridge when the fog lifted just after you pushed Art Jones over the rails. We couldn't risk leaving Ryker alive."

Day said in a brittle tone: "If the police found the bullet the ballistics experts could match the rifling with your gun."

"It no longer exists — I smashed it and buried the remains."

Day breathed relief.

"But that's not all. According to Hank Lee the cops in San Francisco and Vegas are trying to find Art Jones — *after Shand found out about Art Jones knowing Eddie Ryker.*"

"My God!" Day whispered.

Bakso said: "The police up there think it's possible that Art Jones pushed *you* off the bridge and then vanished."

"It could be a short step from that theory to the right one," Day said harshly.

"No way. They don't know that Art Jones was a near double of you and that's the key to everything. Also, they can't possibly know that you and Jones had met before."

"It was a chance encounter on the sidewalk. We were both struck by our mutual resemblance. That gave me the idea. I found out that he was in a jam over money and said I might have a proposition for him if he'd meet me on the bridge the next night when the fog was predicted. He agreed. I put a gun on him, made him wear my blazer and climb the rails and simply pushed him off. After that it all seemed foolproof.

And now this . . . "

Day looked up bleakly. "Is there something else?"

"One other thing. Lee says that Shand found out about Ryker being on the bridge from some broad, a girl named Judy Gresham, who has a small apartment on Laxby Street. Apparently, she was on the bridge, too. The mist blotted out her view. But she did catch a fleeting glimpse of Ryker whom she knew as a jazz musician."

"My God!" said Day again. "How many more people were around at the time without my knowing?"

"There weren't any more. And Ryker can't talk. Nor can Lew Packard, who played the rôle of Albert Fisher — the one thing he did successfully."

Alvin Day said tightly: "I don't like it — sooner or later Shand is going to get on to the truth."

"Yeah, Shand is dangerous." Bakso grinned wolfishly. "Danny didn't like him when he was in the club."

"You mean . . . "

"Danny Schultz is a gunner. He'd take care of Shand — for a consideration."

"No — one slip and the police would trace him back to us. We can't afford that risk."

"Alternatively, I could give a contract to one of the trouble boys."

Day was silent for a long moment. Then he said slowly: "It would be better done a long way from Los Angeles."

"Where, for instance?"

"In San Francisco — at the exact spot on the Golden Gate Bridge where I got rid of Art Jones."

Bakso stared. "How are you going to induce Shand to be there?"

Day didn't answer directly. Instead, he asked: "Do you know where Shand is staying in L.A.?"

"He's at the President Hotel on Wilshire Boulevard — he told me himself."

"Good. So I call him on the telephone saying I'm Art Jones and asking him to meet me on the bridge at ten o'clock tonight as I have something vital to tell him. Only Art Jones won't be there. I'll be there instead — waiting for Mr God Almighty Shand."

"What about your voice? He's already heard you on the telephone."

"I can drastically change it — and speak through a wadded handkerchief."

"We could have one of the staff make the call . . ."

"No, it's better we don't have anyone else in on it."

"Shand is a powerful guy to throw off a bridge, if that's what you're intending."

"It's a simple matter of strategy."

"What if he sees you first?"

"He won't know me even if he has my photograph but I'll know him — I saw him on the closed circuit TV we have the first time he was here. Besides, there's another dense fog over the bridge. It's expected to last several days. I heard it on a radio newscast earlier today."

"It might lift."

"Then we think of something else. But we can check with the San Francisco weather bureau. I'll do it now." Day made the call. When he put the receiver down he said: "Very heavy sea fog expected to persist throughout tonight and tomorrow and probably the day after. That means the chances of people being on the bridge are remote — and even if there are any they won't be able to see more than a few feet."

Bakso mashed his cigarette out. "It's over-elaborate."

"You're forgetting something: I've done it before."

"I still like it better that we deal with Shand here."

"We don't want the L.A. cops milling around. It's out of their hands if he dies in San Francisco — and by the time the body is recovered we'll be long gone." Davy laughed. "Also, it'll be a nice poetic touch."

"All right. You can get the two o'clock flight to San Francisco. I take it the airport there is clear of fog."

"I'll check." Day used the telephone again. Then: "Yes, it's clear. We'll both go. Only you won't be on the bridge — you'll be at the Gresham girl's apartment when she comes in from work. You'll need another gun . . . "

"Yeah," Bakso said.

Day called the President Hotel. When he put the phone down he said: "Shand's not in. I left a message: *Will Mr Dale Shand be on the Golden Gate Bridge in San Francisco at ten p.m. tonight, seventy yards on the bridge at the spot used by Alvin Day. Vital information has come into my possession. — Art Jones.* That'll ensure he's there. On the spot, as Al Capone used to say."

★ ★ ★

I closed the barely open panel flush with the wall and went out the way I had come. I had heard everything . . . and had seen Alvin Day with his new face.

237

15

I CALLED Judy Gresham at her place of work. The woman on the office switchboard answered. "Is it a private call, sir?"

"A personal call from Dale Shand in Los Angeles to Miss Gresham."

The voice became prim. "Members of the staff are not ordinarily allowed to receive private calls."

"I appreciate that, but it's an extraordinary matter of considerable importance and urgency. Can you bend the rule just this one time?"

"Well . . . well, all right then. I'll put you through. Just for a few minutes."

"Thanks."

"You're welcome."

Judy Gresham's voice came on the line. "Why, Dale, how nice to hear you. We're not supposed to take outside calls, but the switchboard operator says this one is important."

"It is — very. What time do you finish work?"

"Four thirty."

"And you go straight home?"

"Yes, but . . . "

"Don't," I said.

"I don't understand. Why not?"

I told her, briefly, adding: "I'm catching a flight to San Francisco, not the one they're taking. The next."

Judy said, calmly: "What am I going to do until you arrive?"

"Take in a movie."

"I could do that. Afterwards I'll wait for you at the Blue Note."

"I should have thought of that myself," I said. I called the airport to book a flight, then got through to Police Headquarters in San Francisco. Bernard Halls was in. He listened without interrupting. Finally, he made a low whistle and said: "If you didn't tape the overheard conversation there's still no concrete proof."

"I'll get it — on the bridge, Captain."

239

"I'll have it staked out."

"Yeah, do that — but keep your men out of sight while I challenge Day."

"You're taking a risk. I don't know that I . . ."

"A calculated risk — and I have the advantage of knowing that he's going to be there. Let me do it this way and we get the kind of proof that'll stand up."

Halls still appeared to hesitate. I said: "If it'll make you feel better be on the bridge near me — not too near but close enough to hear. You'll have the fog cover, unless it lifts."

"It'll not lift this side of tomorrow, most likely not then."

"That's fine."

"As a matter of fact, it's getting worse. Okay, we'll play it your way. I'll have men at both ends of the bridge. I'll also have some at Miss Gresham's apartment, waiting for Bakso to show. They can throw a break-in at him — that'll do as a holding charge."

Halls made a dry kind of sound. "You want to know something? I never did like Bakso. I always felt that he could be a hood in disguise."

I flew to San Francisco and got a taxi to the Blue Note. They were just opening up for the night. I passed a little time nursing a dry martini at the bar.

At 8.25 p.m. Judy Gresham came in, looking for me. I called out: "Over here, Judy."

She walked up to me, smiling. "Dale, it *is* nice to see you."

"Would you like a martini?"

"I would. A white martini, please."

"Did you take in a movie?"

"Yes. I saw a British film, *Murder on the Orient Express*. I liked it, but I kept thinking I was connected with a real murder." She made a small shiver. "It's dangerous what you're going to do, isn't it?"

"Mine's a dangerous business — well, some of the time. Also, I'm usually very well paid."

"No money is big enough if you get killed, Dale."

"Then I'll try to stay alive. Besides,

I can handle this situation — and the police will be nearby."

The club had a small restaurant. I ordered Manhattan steaks. Judy Gresham laughed. "You don't let the prospect of danger spoil your appetite, do you?"

"Nothing spoils my appetite," I said cheerfully.

She hesitated, then said: "I suppose I mustn't go on the bridge with you?"

"That's right, you mustn't."

"I'll wait here."

"It's as good a place as any. In fact, better than most. I may be late, but they stay open until the small hours — and I'll be here, Judy."

"I'll wait, no matter how long. But don't tell me not to worry — because I will, every minute until you come back."

"Everything's going to be all right," I said, adding silently: At least, I hope it is.

"When it's all over what are you going to do?"

"I've got two weeks of my vacation left. I thought of visiting Disneyland and after that going up to the Grand Canyon, maybe losing a little money in Vegas, then looking round San Francisco on the way back to L.A. and home.

"I could act as your guide to San Francisco, if you like."

"I like, but how about your job?"

"By the happiest of coincidences I have two weeks holiday starting tomorrow. I could . . . " She didn't finish the sentence.

I did. "You could come on holiday with me for the entire two weeks, Judy."

"Yes, I could."

"I'm putting in a formal request — will you?"

"Yes, Dale."

"It's asking a lot. I might make a pass at you."

"You might," she said calmly.

"Suppose I did?"

"I'll cross *that* bridge when we come

to it. By the way, Bill Rush — the man I told you about — wants to marry me."

"So?"

"Yes, he called to see me at lunchtime today and asked me."

"A bit sudden, wasn't it?"

"Not altogether. I sensed he was attracted when we met the first time."

"And you?"

"He's a nice guy, but I'm not in love with him. In fact, I don't want to marry anyone right now or even in the foreseeable future."

"But you're willing to go on a vacation trip with me?"

"Yes — I like you." Her eyes were very clear as she said it.

"It's mutual, Judy," I said.

I left her just before 9.30 p.m. and taxied to the bridge. I squinted at my watch. Twelve minutes to deadline. Maybe Alvin Day was already there? I stepped on to the bridge. Something moved in the almost opaque fog. Then a burred voice said: "Mr Shand?"

"Yeah." I half drew my gun from its shoulder clip. But it wasn't Day. A plain-clothes detective.

"Burnet, detective sergeant. Okay, Captain Halls is already on the bridge. You won't see him, but he's there."

"Thanks."

"Good luck, Mr Shand."

I moved forward without haste, calculating the exact distance to the spot where Art Jones fell to his death. A dozen more paces and I would be there. Instead, I veered at an angle and stopped, motionless.

Now only a handful of seconds were left. I took out the gun and freed the safety catch.

A sound, minimal and muffled by the encompassing fog, but I heard it. A figure loomed, no more than yards away. A man. It had to be Alvin Day. Better be sure, though. I was sure when he swept his right hand inside his swung-open jacket and came out with a .357 Magnum. Three times deadlier than the traditional .38 Smith and Wesson. If you use it first.

I stepped soundlessly sideways, said: "To paraphrase a historic greeting — Mr Alvin Day, I presume?"

The man who had been leaning against the parapet, jerked convulsively, then stopped in a frozen travesty of arrested motion.

"*Shand!*" The name came in an ascending scream.

"Or perhaps you would prefer to be known as Art Jones — for this occasion only."

"You . . . " He struggled for words, found none.

"Only Art Jones died among the sharks after you pushed him off the bridge and now he's a heap of ashes labelled Alvin Day."

His hand moved.

I said: "Don't try to bring that big cannon up, my friend — there's a gun already looking at you."

I could see him clearly now, there were no more than a few feet between us. His eyes glared. There was a mad sickness in them. He tongued his lips. "How . . . "

I finished the strangled question for him. "How did I know you with the transformed face? The answer is that I didn't recognize you — Hemsley made one swell job with the cosmetic surgery."

"You know that, too . . . "

"Yeah, I know. Also, you had to be Day — a man on the bridge, with a gun, at this exact spot and this exact time. Just as you planned it today with Bakso."

Day said, whisperingly: "You know too goddam much, Shand . . . too much to go on living."

"I got into your club at noon today and heard everything — but I already knew you had murdered Art Jones, an innocent man who had the misfortune to be a ringer for you, so that you could completely switch your identity."

"You can't prove . . . " Day suddenly stopped.

I went on: "Art Jones — the guy

you killed, the guy who was wrongly identified as you — had all his own teeth. Your wife says you have a partial lower denture. I guess that ought to be conclusive."

Day laughed madly. The laugh ended and he said in a deadly voice: "So I killed Jones — sure I killed him. I didn't bear him any ill-will. He meant nothing to me. But I knew when we first met that I was going to kill him. It was logically inevitable, a necessary piece of the grand strategy. I had to do it, I tell you I had to do it . . . "

I said nothing.

"It was the perfect crime, everything meticulously worked out. I even made him wear my watch and ring, here on the bridge . . . and but for you . . . " Day screamed again. Then, quietly: "But you're not going to prove it, Shand. They'd say I was a psycho and shut me up in a madhouse and I'm not . . . "

As he spoke Day lunged violently

sideways, bringing the Magnum up and out.

I fired. The big gun slid from his hand, skittering across the bridge. He wheeled, started climbing the rails. I pelted forward as a posse of police, led by Halls, swept in. I reached the rails first, clawing for Day's jacket, just missing it.

Simultaneously, a risen wind from the ocean lifted the fog. Day was silhouetted against the suddenly clear night sky, swaying with the upper part of his body grotesquely far out. Then he jumped, going down, down from the bridge. He screamed one more time, a high keening dissonance which hung in the air before it died with him.

Halls looked at the swirling water two hundred and sixty-three feet below. "So he jumped off the bridge at the finish . . . "

"Yeah — the last leap," I said.

* * *

249

It was just past midnight when I got back to the Blue Note and told Judy what had happened.

"So it's all over," she said. "Above all, you're safe."

"In another sense it's not quite all over for me, Judy — I have to make a statement in the morning and attend the coroner's inquiry. Meanwhile, the police have arrested Bakso — he broke into your apartment, waiting for you to show."

"But for you I'd have been there . . . "

I said: "I'll see you home. We can get a taxi."

"I came in my car. I'll drive us there."

The drive was short. She led the way into the kitchen, turned and said: "Are you hungry?"

"I don't think so. In fact, I'm not."

"Nor me. But you have the look of a man in need of a drink. I'll join you." She fixed two old-fashioneds. We walked them into the cosy living-room.

"So Alvin Day committed suicide after all," she said.

"Yes."

"All his grandiose plans came to nothing — thanks to you."

"I'll have to go back to Pasadena later tomorrow — or rather, today. I'll have to tell Larraine Day."

"It's better that she hears it from you, Dale."

I said: "We'll catch the late afternoon flight to L.A. After I've seen Larraine Day we put the whole thing behind us and go off on holiday."

"Yes," she said.

I grinned faintly. "Taking this case brought some wholly unexpected results."

"Yes, it brought you me . . . "

I circled an arm round her waist, aware of her nearness, all the soft warm femininity of her.

Suddenly, she said: "Are you booked into an hotel?"

"Hell, I completely forgot to do it. I'll call one now."

"Don't bother. You can stay here."

"You have a spare room?"

She shook her head.

"I can sleep on the davenport."

She wound both arms round my neck, standing on her toes. "Don't bother," she said again.

16

IT was the next evening when I drove out to the house on the gentle knoll over in Pasadena, the brownstone house which looked as if it properly belonged in New York's East Seventies. I remembered the crazy idea I had had about it. But the idea wasn't half so crazy as the macabre reality of what had happened since.

Larraine Day opened the door herself. She looked cool and composed in tapered navy slacks and a sheer white shirt-blouse with a pointed collar, but her eyes betrayed the inner sadness which possessed her.

"Captain Halls of the San Francisco police telephoned me," she said. "It seems my husband's body was taken from the sea last night, not weeks ago. He said you would tell me everything."

"Yes, your husband committed

suicide, Mrs Day. Last night, not several weeks ago. The body which was identified as your husband's was that of a man named Art Jones — a man who was almost his exact double."

Her clasped hands tightened, so that the knuckles showed whitely. "Are you telling me that Alvin deliberately allowed this man's body to be identified as his?"

I shifted my weight in a chair, reflecting that what I had to say was the hardest part of the case. But there was no easy way out.

I said levelly: "Your husband was secretly forming a syndicate — a crime syndicate in partnership with Bakso, the ex-cop from San Francisco. He met Art Jones by sheer chance on a previous visit to San Francisco. The extraordinary resemblance gave him the idea."

"What idea?" The whispered words only just reached me.

"Your husband wanted a total change of identity. He got this man to meet

254

him on the Golden Gate Bridge and pushed him off it, having first induced Jones to wear some of his clothes which contained some of your husband's personal belongings. In the event Art Jones was assumed to be Alvin Day."

Larraine Day said: "Dear God . . . "

"The identification was made in good faith by George Lane — they spared you having to see the body which had been mutilated by sharks. Identification was the major step. Then your husband had his face changed by cosmetic surgery. This was done by a crooked surgeon from San Diego. With a new face, tinted hair and a moustache the change was virtually total. He ceased to be Alvin Day."

A tremor ran through her. Then it was gone and she said: "So Alvin committed suicide — but at a different time."

"At twenty minutes after ten o'clock last night — on the Golden Gate Bridge. He leaped off it. I tried to stop him, but I was too late." I told her how I came to be there and I told her all the rest of the story.

For minutes she said nothing, sitting without movement or expression. In the total silence the ticking of the ornate mantel clock sounded almost strident.

Then she said in a low voice: "All the time you were investigating the case I was frightened. Not about what you've told me — I suspected nothing like that. I started to wonder if Alvin had another woman or women. I thought he might have been blackmailed . . . or murdered."

"No, it wasn't like that," I lied. I was thinking of Mitzi Bellson and the small deception I was guilty of in not telling. There was a reason. I heard myself putting it into words. "Until this happened you had a happy marriage, Larraine."

She looked up. "Yes, it was very, very happy. Even now I find it hard to believe that Alvin did this dreadful thing . . . something must have happened to him. I'll try not to think about it. I'll try to remember only the happiness we shared."

I stood up. She walked with me to the door. She looked at me for a long moment and said unexpectedly: "I'm glad you couldn't pull him back . . . "

★ ★ ★

I drove back to L.A. Judy was waiting in the hotel lounge. I had only just joined her when Halls came on the telephone.

"Some kids found Bakso's smashed gun while they were playing in Lincoln Park. It was buried behind a clump of bushes. A chance in a thousand. He used a .38. The rifling matches the slug which killed Eddie Ryker. So he faces a Murder One rap."

"They had to kill Ryker because he knew Art Jones," I said. "The one thing that bugs me is how Bakso knew Ryker was on the bridge that night."

Halls said: "We've cleared that up.

Apparently, Ryker saw two men near the rails — they would be Day and Jones. He didn't see them clearly. But later, after the publicity in the media, he decided to tell the police in case it was significant. One of the civilian clerks working at Police Headquarters remembers him coming in about it. Unfortunately, Ryker was routed to Bakso."

"Unfortunate for Eddie Ryker. Incidentally, how did Bakso come to kill Ryker in that musical instruments store he ran?"

"Bakso isn't saying. In fact, he isn't saying anything about anything — but we're pretty damn sure he arranged to see Ryker there after writing those two goodbye notes with his left hand. He *had* to see Ryker in a place where they would be alone — the music shop late at night was the perfect spot for the murder. Meanwhile, Bakso is hiring a sky-priced lawyer. It'll not save him," Halls added grimly.

"Finding Bakso's buried gun ought

to be more than enough to go before a Grand Jury," I said.

"Yes, it's a police positive issued to him when he was a cop. He claimed he had handed it in when he quit and forged a receipt to that effect, which was a mistake."

"Even Homer nodded. Did your men find him actually in Judy Gresham's apartment?"

"Yeah — and he's going to be hard put to explain *that*." Halls paused, then said: "I guess he'd have killed her but for you, Shand. She knew too much, or he figured she knew. There's one other thing — Alvin Day would've faced a Murder One rap if you'd been able to stop him going off the bridge."

I didn't speak.

"I've been doing some thinking about that," Halls said. "You want to know what I think?"

"You're going to tell me, anyway, aren't you?"

"I think you could have stopped him going over the side if you'd wanted to."

"Are you going to slap a charge on me?"

Halls made a dry sound. "I've no proof, just the thought. Maybe it's better he went the way he did."

"It's better," I said.

THE END

Other titles in the Linford Mystery Library:

A GENTEEL LITTLE MURDER
Philip Daniels

Gilbert had a long-cherished plan to murder his wife. When the polished Edward entered the scene Gilbert's attitude was suddenly changed.

DEATH AT THE WEDDING
Madelaine Duke

Dr. Norah North's search for a killer takes her from a wedding to a private hospital.

MURDER FIRST CLASS
Ron Ellis

Will Detective Chief Inspector Glass find the Post Office robbers before the Executioner gets to them?

THE DRACULA MURDERS
Philip Daniels

The Horror Ball was interrupted by a spectral figure who warned the merrymakers they were tampering with the unknown.

THE LADIES
OF LAMBTON GREEN
Liza Shepherd

Why did murdered Robin Colquhoun's picture pose such a threat to the ladies of Lambton Green?

CARNABY
AND THE GAOLBREAKERS
Peter N. Walker

Detective Sergeant James Aloysius Carnaby-King is sent to prison as bait. When he joins in an escape he is thrown headfirst into a vicious murder hunt.

STORM CENTRE
Douglas Clark

Detective Chief Superintendent Masters, temporarily lecturing in a police staff college, finds there's more to the job than a few weeks relaxation in a rural setting.

THE MANUSCRIPT MURDERS
Roy Harley Lewis

Antiquarian bookseller Matthew Coll, acquires a rare 16th century manuscript. But when the Dutch professor who had discovered the journal is murdered, Coll begins to doubt its authenticity.

SHARENDEL
Margaret Carr

Ruth didn't want all that money. And she didn't want Aunt Cass to die. But at Sharendel things looked different. She began to wonder if she had a split personality.

A FOOT IN THE GRAVE
Bruce Marshall

About to be imprisoned and tortured in Buenos Aires, John Smith escapes, only to become involved in an aeroplane hijacking.

DEAD TROUBLE
Martin Carroll

Trespassing brought Jennifer Denning more than she bargained for. She was totally unprepared for the violence which was to lie in her path.

HOURS TO KILL
Ursula Curtiss

Margaret went to New Mexico to look after her sick sister's rented house and felt a sharp edge of fear when the absent landlady arrived.

MUD IN HIS EYE
Gerald Hammond

The harbourmaster's body is found mangled beneath Major Smyle's yacht. What is the sinister significance of the illicit oysters?

THE SCAVENGERS
Bill Knox

Among the masses of struggling fish in the *Tecta*'s nets was a larger, darker, ominously motionless form . . . the body of a skin diver.

DEATH IN ARCADY
Stella Phillips

Detective Inspector Matthew Furnival works unofficially with the local police when a brutal murder takes place in a caravan camp.

THE DEATH OF ABBE DIDIER
Richard Grayson

Inspector Gautier of the Sûreté investigates three crimes which are strangely connected.

NIGHTMARE TIME
Hugh Pentecost

Have the missing major and his wife met with foul play somewhere in the Beaumont Hotel, or is their disappearance a carefully planned step in an act of treason?

BLOOD WILL OUT
Margaret Carr

Why was the manor house so oddly familiar to Elinor Howard? Who would have guessed that a Sunday School outing could lead to murder?